William Shakespeare's
A Midsummer Night's Dream

adapted by **Dan Conner**
illustrated by **Rod Espinosa**

magic wagon

Published by Magic Wagon, a division of the ABDO Publishing Group, 8000 West 78th Street, Edina, Minnesota 55439. Copyright © 2009 by Abdo Consulting Group, Inc. International copyrights reserved in all countries. All rights reserved. No part of this book may be reproduced in any form without written permission from the publisher.
Graphic Planet™ is a trademark and logo of Magic Wagon.

Printed in the United States.

Adapted by Dan Conner
Illustrated by Rod Espinosa
Edited by Stephanie Hedlund and Rochelle Baltzer
Interior layout and design by Antarctic Press
Cover art by Rod Espinosa
Cover design by Neil Klinepier

Library of Congress Cataloging-in-Publication Data

Conner, Daniel, 1985-
  William Shakespeare's A midsummer night's dream / adapted by Daniel Conner ;
illustrated by Rod Espinosa.
     p. cm. -- (Graphic Shakespeare)
  Summary: Retells, in comic book format, Shakespeare's play about the strange events that take place in a forest inhabited by fairies who magically transform the romantic fate of two young couples.
  ISBN 978-1-60270-191-5
  1. Graphic novels. [1. Graphic novels. 2. Shakespeare, William, 1564-1616--Adaptations. 3. Youths' writings.] I. Espinosa, Rod, ill. II. Shakespeare, William, 1564-1616. Midsummer night's dream. III. Title. IV. Title: Midsummer night's dream.
  PZ7.7.C66Wi 2008
  741.5'973--dc22
                                                          2008010745

Table of Contents

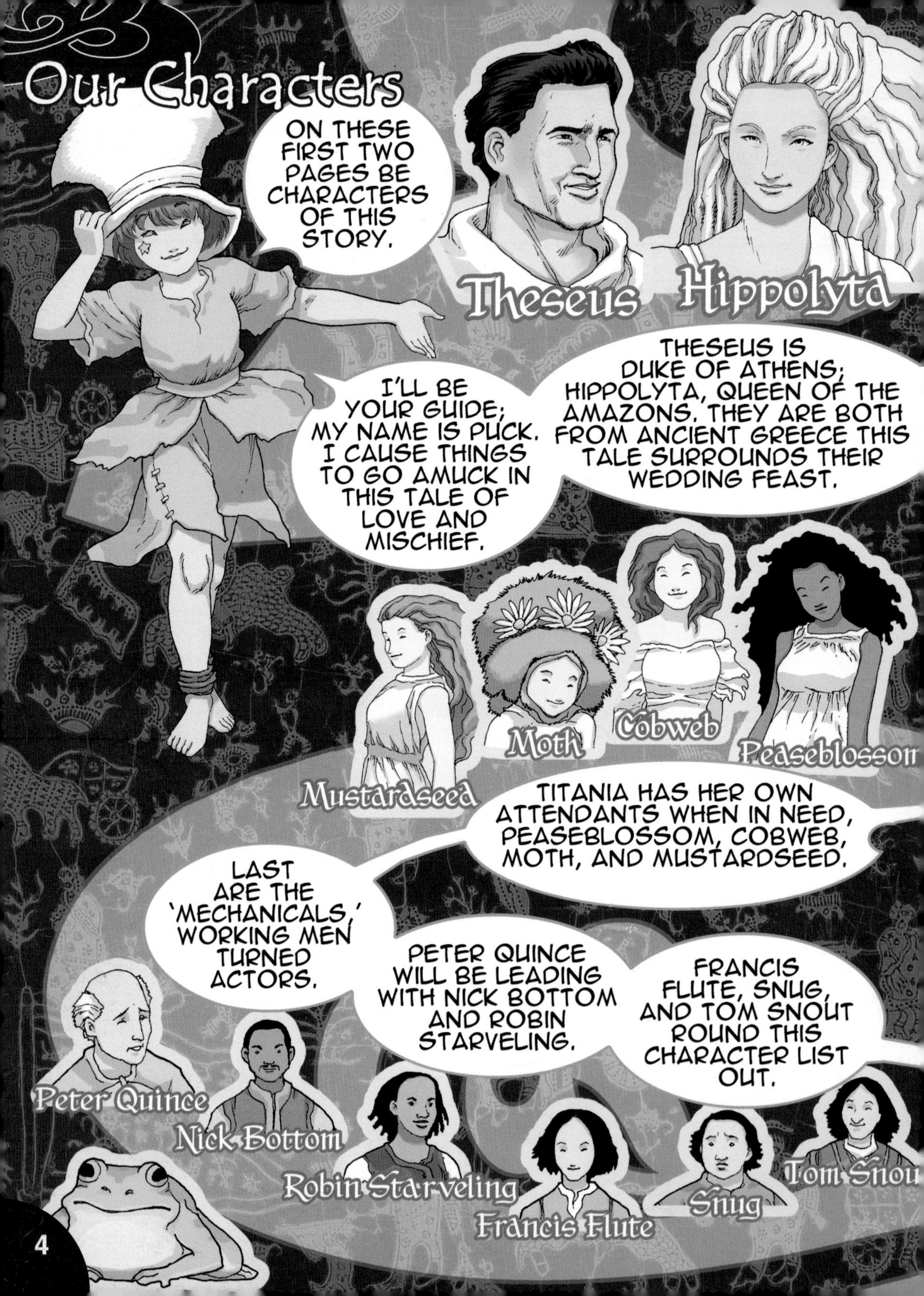

Our Characters
ON THESE FIRST TWO PAGES BE CHARACTERS OF THIS STORY.
Theseus
Hippolyta
I'LL BE YOUR GUIDE; MY NAME IS PUCK. I CAUSE THINGS TO GO AMUCK IN THIS TALE OF LOVE AND MISCHIEF.
THESEUS IS DUKE OF ATHENS; HIPPOLYTA, QUEEN OF THE AMAZONS. THEY ARE BOTH FROM ANCIENT GREECE THIS TALE SURROUNDS THEIR WEDDING FEAST.
Moth
Cobweb
Peaseblossom
Mustardseed
TITANIA HAS HER OWN ATTENDANTS WHEN IN NEED, PEASEBLOSSOM, COBWEB, MOTH, AND MUSTARDSEED.
LAST ARE THE 'MECHANICALS,' WORKING MEN TURNED ACTORS.
PETER QUINCE WILL BE LEADING WITH NICK BOTTOM AND ROBIN STARVELING.
FRANCIS FLUTE, SNUG, AND TOM SNOUT ROUND THIS CHARACTER LIST OUT.
Peter Quince
Nick Bottom
Robin Starveling
Francis Flute
Snug
Tom Snout

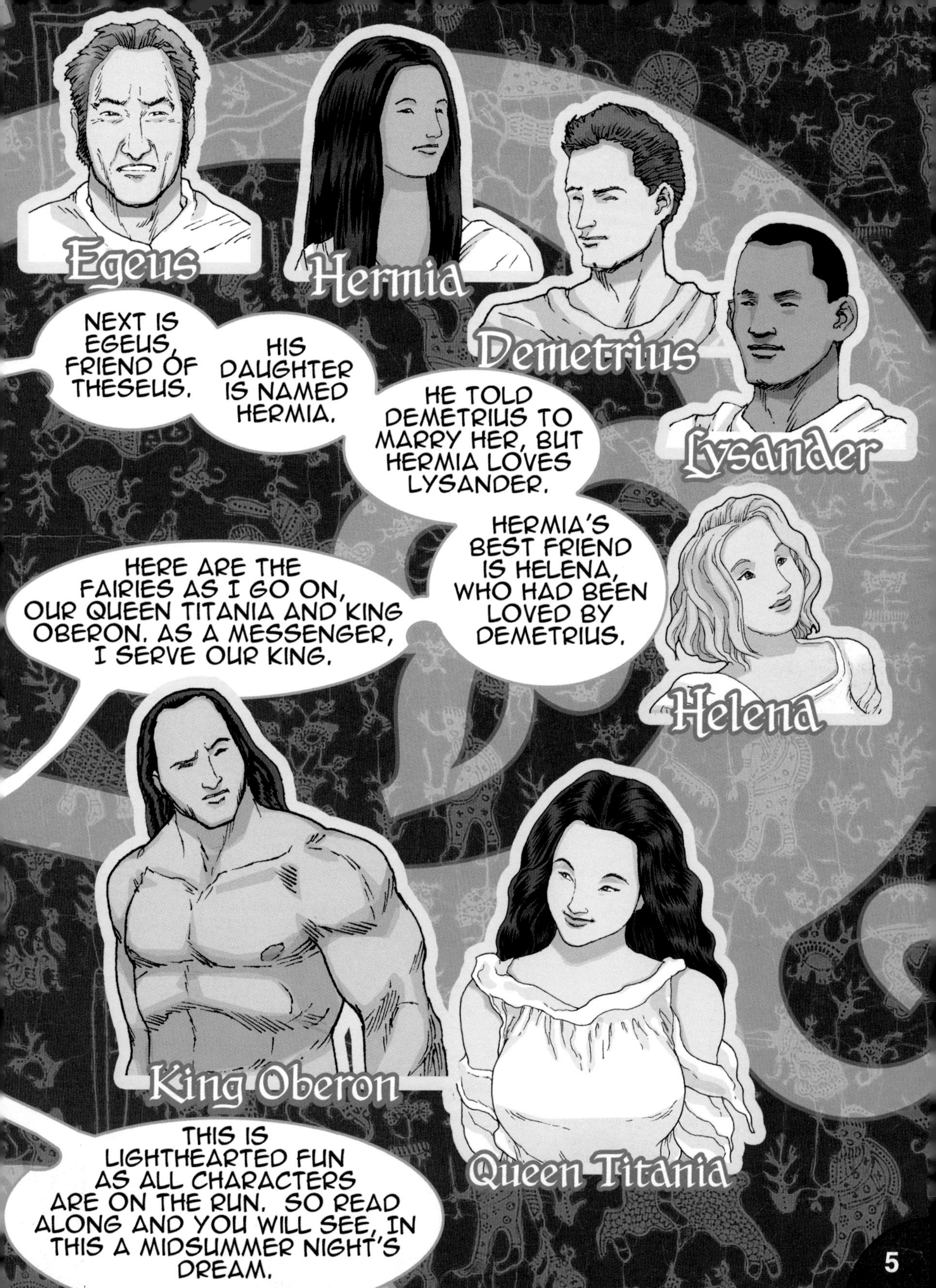
Egeus
Hermia
Demetrius
Lysander
NEXT IS EGEUS, FRIEND OF THESEUS.
HIS DAUGHTER IS NAMED HERMIA.
HE TOLD DEMETRIUS TO MARRY HER, BUT HERMIA LOVES LYSANDER.
HERMIA'S BEST FRIEND IS HELENA, WHO HAD BEEN LOVED BY DEMETRIUS.
Helena
HERE ARE THE FAIRIES AS I GO ON, OUR QUEEN TITANIA AND KING OBERON. AS A MESSENGER, I SERVE OUR KING.
King Oberon
Queen Titania
THIS IS LIGHTHEARTED FUN AS ALL CHARACTERS ARE ON THE RUN. SO READ ALONG AND YOU WILL SEE, IN THIS A MIDSUMMER NIGHT'S DREAM.

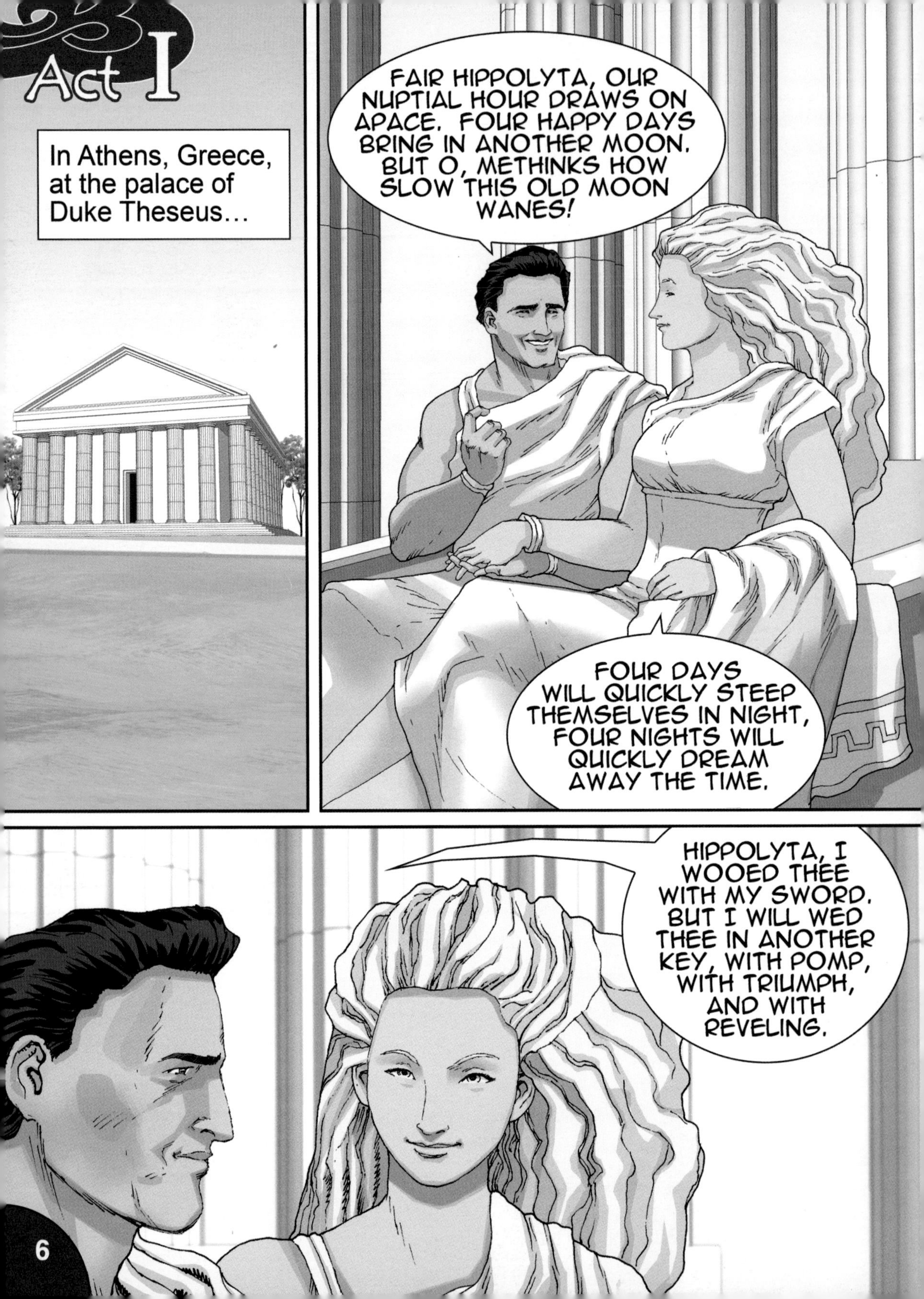
Act I
In Athens, Greece, at the palace of Duke Theseus…
FAIR HIPPOLYTA, OUR NUPTIAL HOUR DRAWS ON APACE. FOUR HAPPY DAYS BRING IN ANOTHER MOON. BUT O, METHINKS HOW SLOW THIS OLD MOON WANES!
FOUR DAYS WILL QUICKLY STEEP THEMSELVES IN NIGHT, FOUR NIGHTS WILL QUICKLY DREAM AWAY THE TIME.
HIPPOLYTA, I WOOED THEE WITH MY SWORD. BUT I WILL WED THEE IN ANOTHER KEY, WITH POMP, WITH TRIUMPH, AND WITH REVELING.

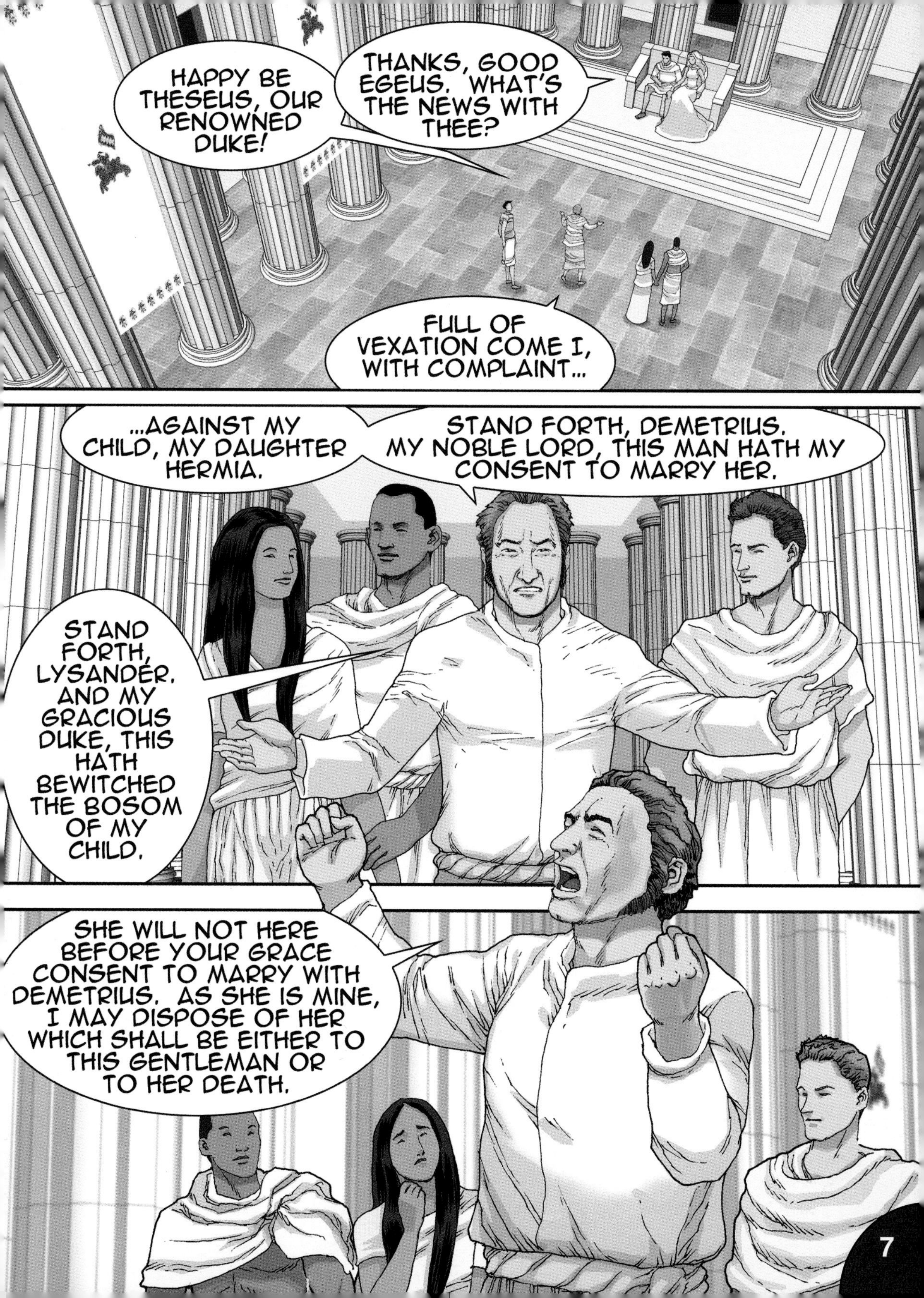
HAPPY BE THESEUS, OUR RENOWNED DUKE!
THANKS, GOOD EGEUS. WHAT'S THE NEWS WITH THEE?
FULL OF VEXATION COME I, WITH COMPLAINT...
...AGAINST MY CHILD, MY DAUGHTER HERMIA.
STAND FORTH, DEMETRIUS. MY NOBLE LORD, THIS MAN HATH MY CONSENT TO MARRY HER.
STAND FORTH, LYSANDER. AND MY GRACIOUS DUKE, THIS HATH BEWITCHED THE BOSOM OF MY CHILD.
SHE WILL NOT HERE BEFORE YOUR GRACE CONSENT TO MARRY WITH DEMETRIUS. AS SHE IS MINE, I MAY DISPOSE OF HER WHICH SHALL BE EITHER TO THIS GENTLEMAN OR TO HER DEATH.

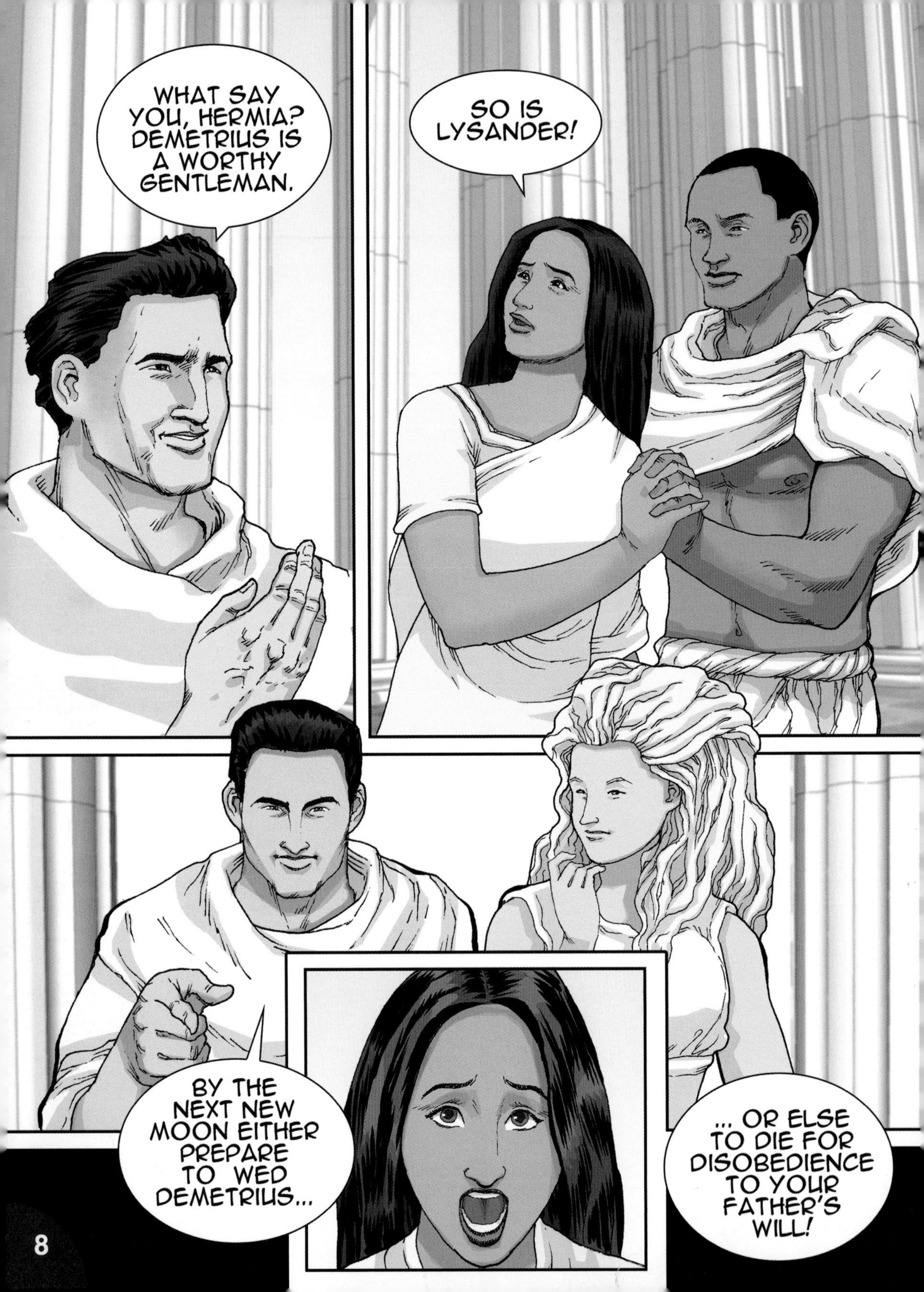
WHAT SAY YOU, HERMIA? DEMETRIUS IS A WORTHY GENTLEMAN.
SO IS LYSANDER!
BY THE NEXT NEW MOON EITHER PREPARE TO WED DEMETRIUS...
... OR ELSE TO DIE FOR DISOBEDIENCE TO YOUR FATHER'S WILL!

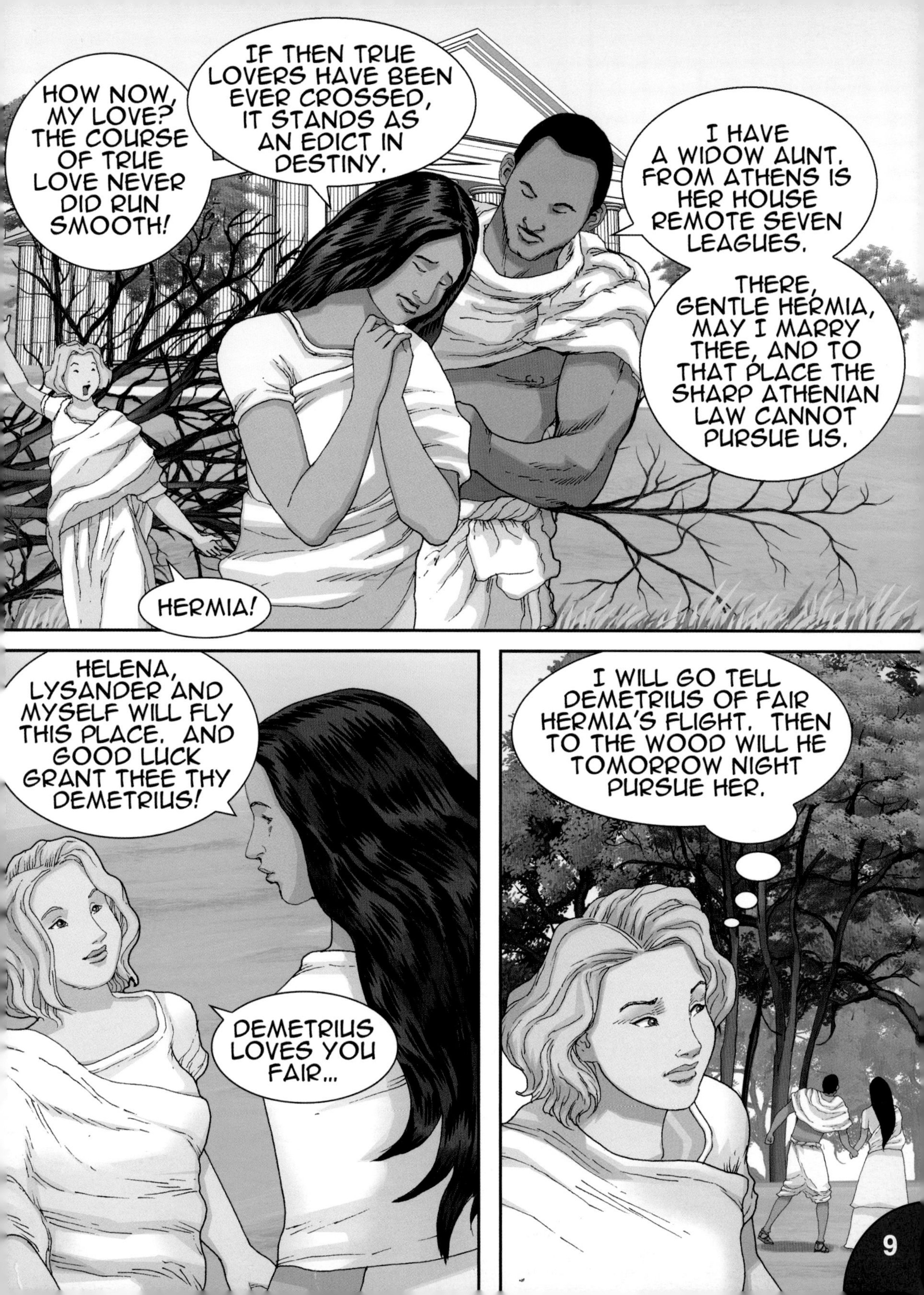
HOW NOW, MY LOVE? THE COURSE OF TRUE LOVE NEVER DID RUN SMOOTH!
IF THEN TRUE LOVERS HAVE BEEN EVER CROSSED, IT STANDS AS AN EDICT IN DESTINY.
I HAVE A WIDOW AUNT. FROM ATHENS IS HER HOUSE REMOTE SEVEN LEAGUES.
THERE, GENTLE HERMIA, MAY I MARRY THEE, AND TO THAT PLACE THE SHARP ATHENIAN LAW CANNOT PURSUE US.
HERMIA!
HELENA, LYSANDER AND MYSELF WILL FLY THIS PLACE. AND GOOD LUCK GRANT THEE THY DEMETRIUS!
DEMETRIUS LOVES YOU FAIR...
I WILL GO TELL DEMETRIUS OF FAIR HERMIA'S FLIGHT. THEN TO THE WOOD WILL HE TOMORROW NIGHT PURSUE HER.

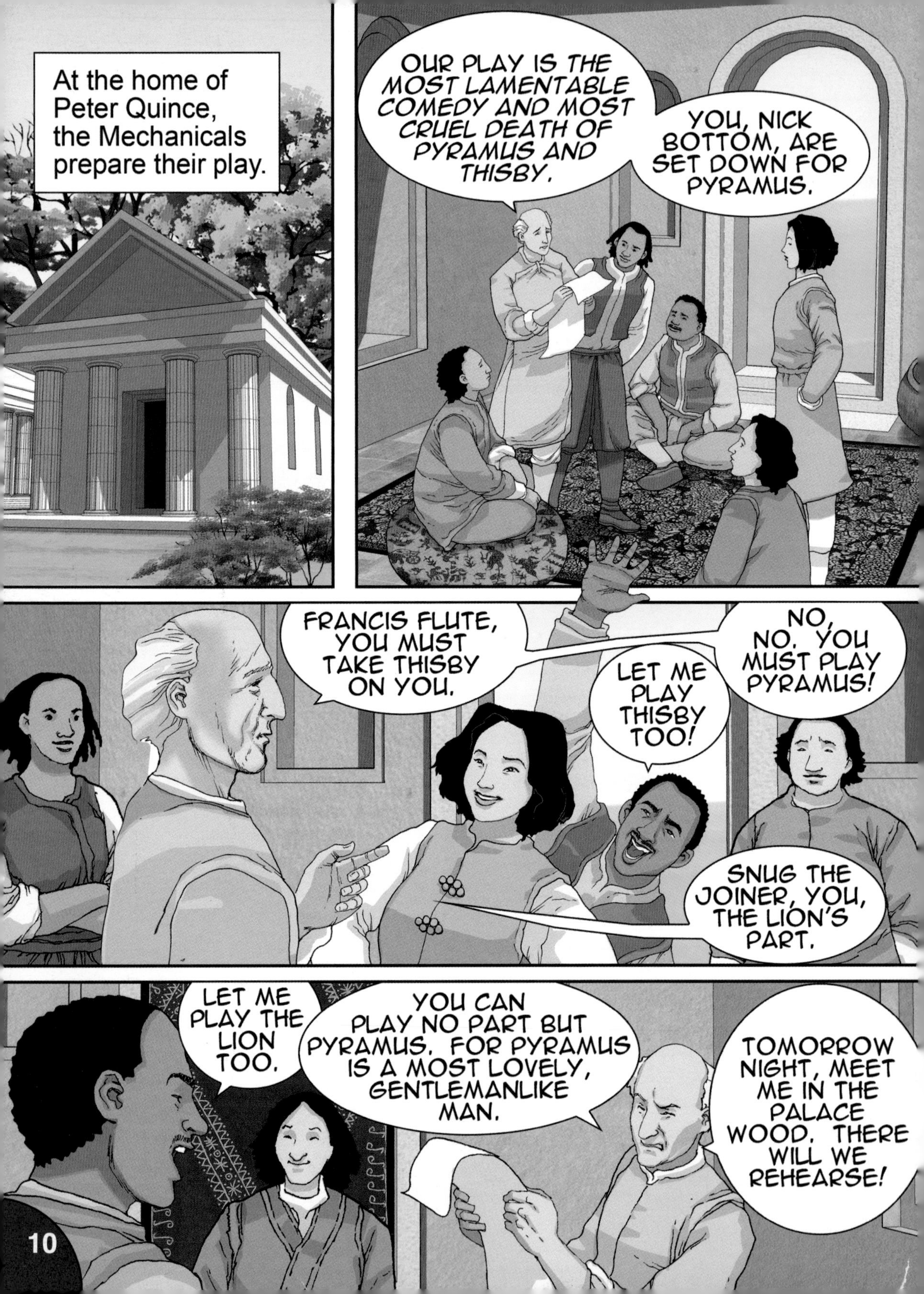
At the home of Peter Quince, the Mechanicals prepare their play.
OUR PLAY IS THE MOST LAMENTABLE COMEDY AND MOST CRUEL DEATH OF PYRAMUS AND THISBY.
YOU, NICK BOTTOM, ARE SET DOWN FOR PYRAMUS.
FRANCIS FLUTE, YOU MUST TAKE THISBY ON YOU.
LET ME PLAY THISBY TOO!
NO, NO. YOU MUST PLAY PYRAMUS!
SNUG THE JOINER, YOU, THE LION'S PART.
LET ME PLAY THE LION TOO.
YOU CAN PLAY NO PART BUT PYRAMUS. FOR PYRAMUS IS A MOST LOVELY, GENTLEMANLIKE MAN.
TOMORROW NIGHT, MEET ME IN THE PALACE WOOD. THERE WILL WE REHEARSE!

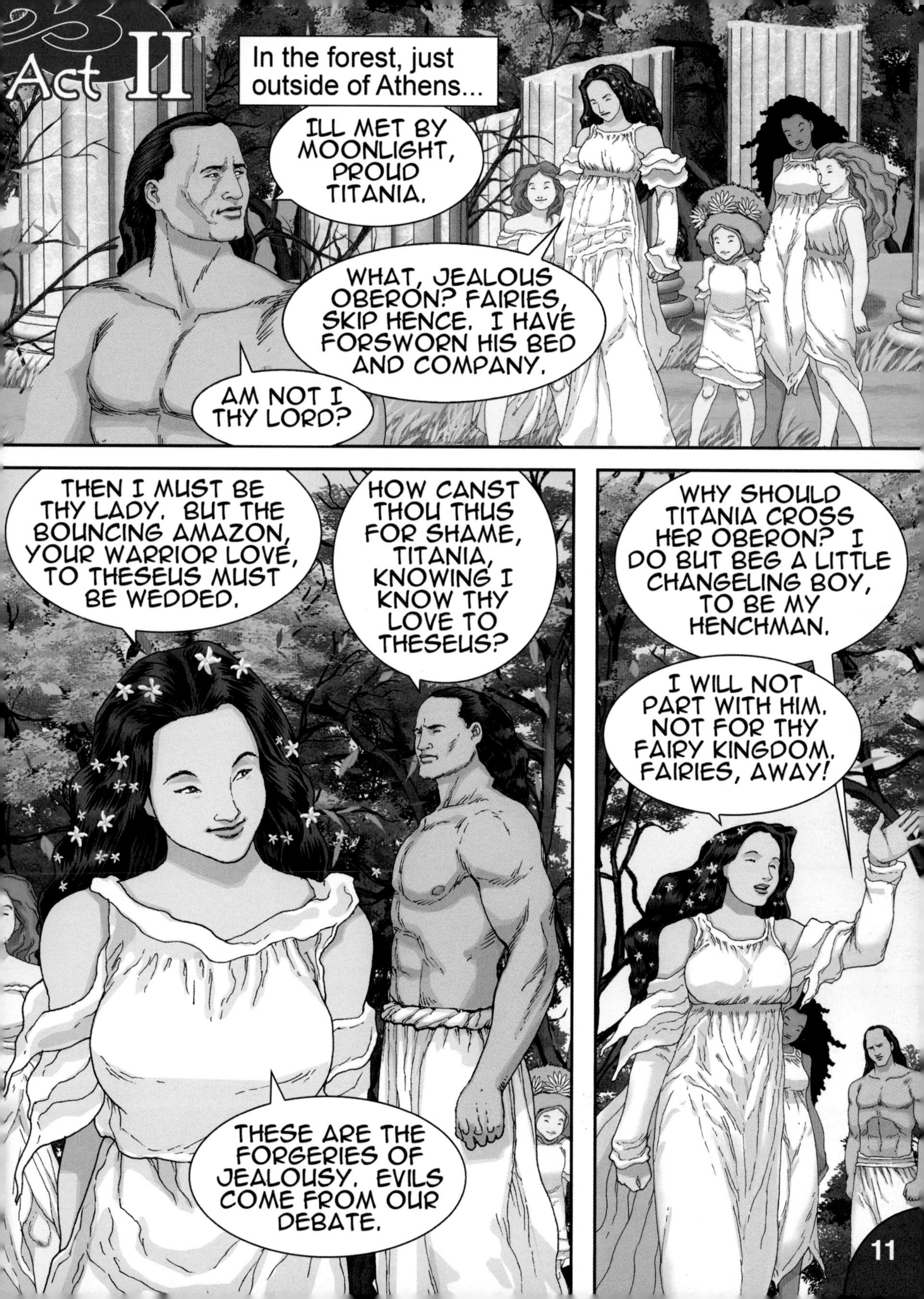
Act II
In the forest, just outside of Athens...
ILL MET BY MOONLIGHT, PROUD TITANIA.
WHAT, JEALOUS OBERON? FAIRIES, SKIP HENCE. I HAVE FORSWORN HIS BED AND COMPANY.
AM NOT I THY LORD?
THEN I MUST BE THY LADY. BUT THE BOUNCING AMAZON, YOUR WARRIOR LOVE, TO THESEUS MUST BE WEDDED.
HOW CANST THOU THUS FOR SHAME, TITANIA, KNOWING I KNOW THY LOVE TO THESEUS?
THESE ARE THE FORGERIES OF JEALOUSY. EVILS COME FROM OUR DEBATE.
WHY SHOULD TITANIA CROSS HER OBERON? I DO BUT BEG A LITTLE CHANGELING BOY, TO BE MY HENCHMAN.
I WILL NOT PART WITH HIM. NOT FOR THY FAIRY KINGDOM. FAIRIES, AWAY!

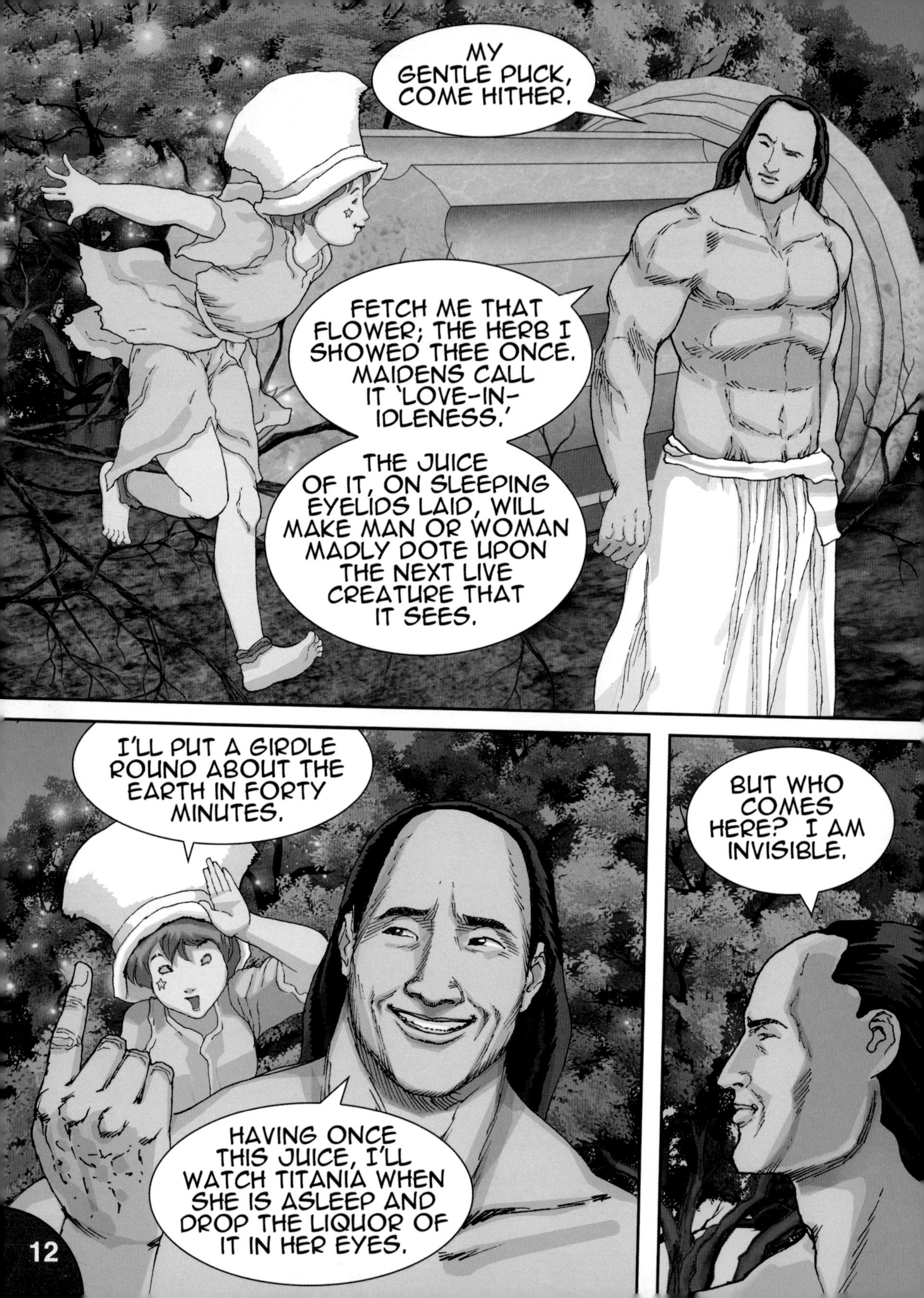
MY GENTLE PUCK, COME HITHER.
FETCH ME THAT FLOWER; THE HERB I SHOWED THEE ONCE. MAIDENS CALL IT 'LOVE-IN-IDLENESS.'
THE JUICE OF IT, ON SLEEPING EYELIDS LAID, WILL MAKE MAN OR WOMAN MADLY DOTE UPON THE NEXT LIVE CREATURE THAT IT SEES.
I'LL PUT A GIRDLE ROUND ABOUT THE EARTH IN FORTY MINUTES.
HAVING ONCE THIS JUICE, I'LL WATCH TITANIA WHEN SHE IS ASLEEP AND DROP THE LIQUOR OF IT IN HER EYES.
BUT WHO COMES HERE? I AM INVISIBLE.

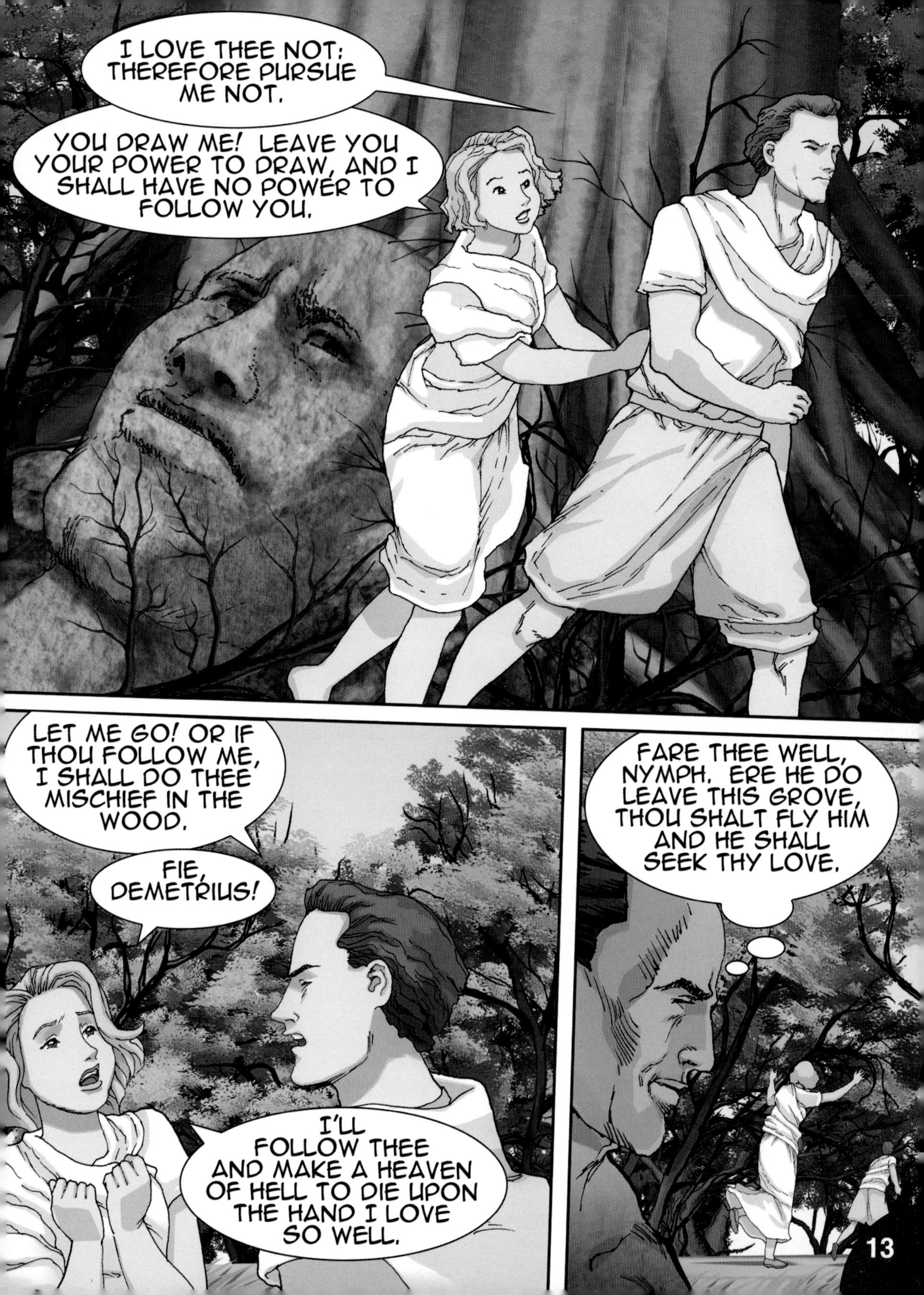
I LOVE THEE NOT: THEREFORE PURSUE ME NOT.
YOU DRAW ME! LEAVE YOU YOUR POWER TO DRAW, AND I SHALL HAVE NO POWER TO FOLLOW YOU.
LET ME GO! OR IF THOU FOLLOW ME, I SHALL DO THEE MISCHIEF IN THE WOOD.
FIE, DEMETRIUS!
I'LL FOLLOW THEE AND MAKE A HEAVEN OF HELL TO DIE UPON THE HAND I LOVE SO WELL.
FARE THEE WELL, NYMPH. ERE HE DO LEAVE THIS GROVE, THOU SHALT FLY HIM AND HE SHALL SEEK THY LOVE.

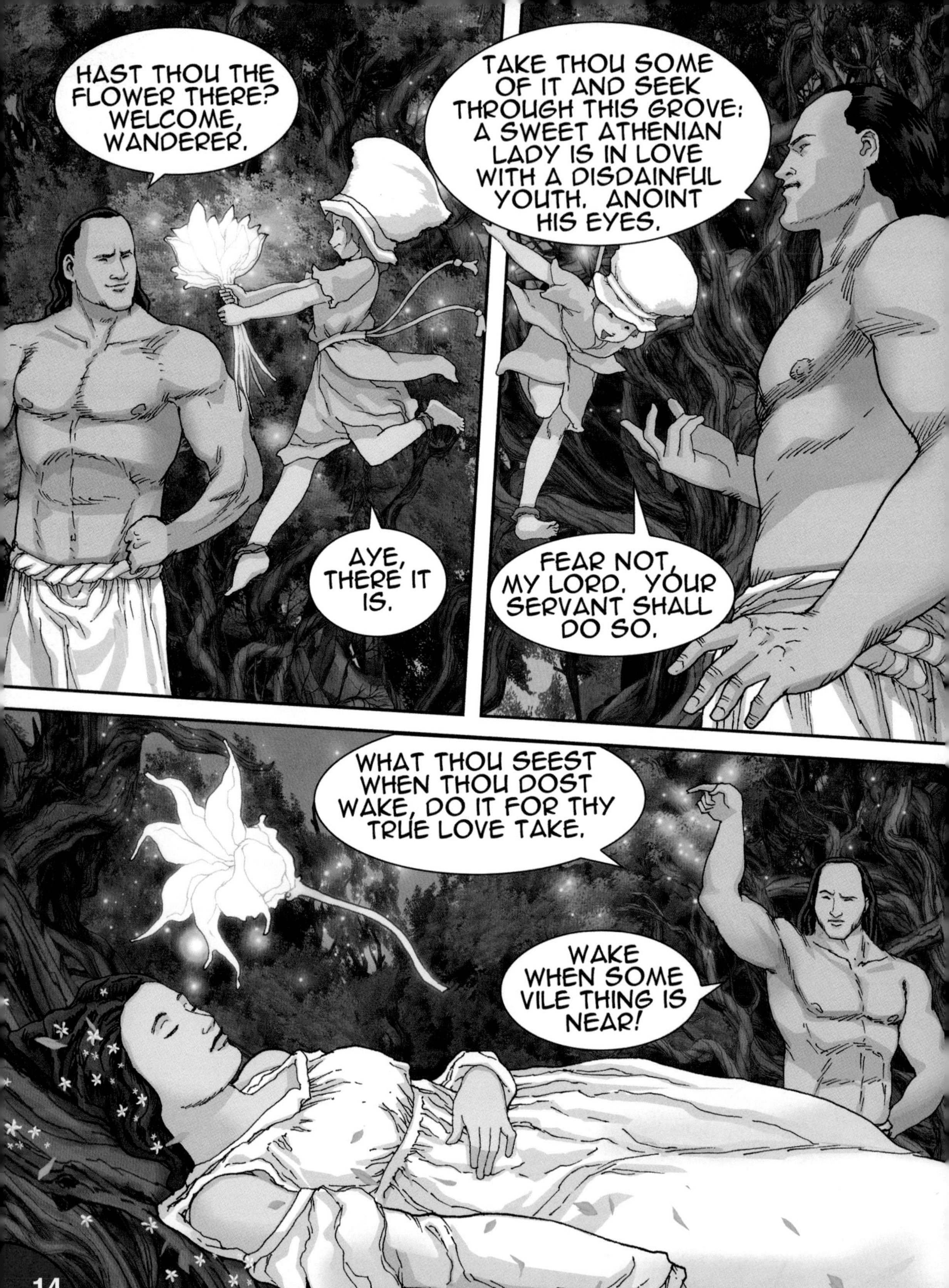
HAST THOU THE FLOWER THERE? WELCOME, WANDERER.
AYE, THERE IT IS.
TAKE THOU SOME OF IT AND SEEK THROUGH THIS GROVE: A SWEET ATHENIAN LADY IS IN LOVE WITH A DISDAINFUL YOUTH. ANOINT HIS EYES.
FEAR NOT, MY LORD. YOUR SERVANT SHALL DO SO.
WHAT THOU SEEST WHEN THOU DOST WAKE, DO IT FOR THY TRUE LOVE TAKE.
WAKE WHEN SOME VILE THING IS NEAR!

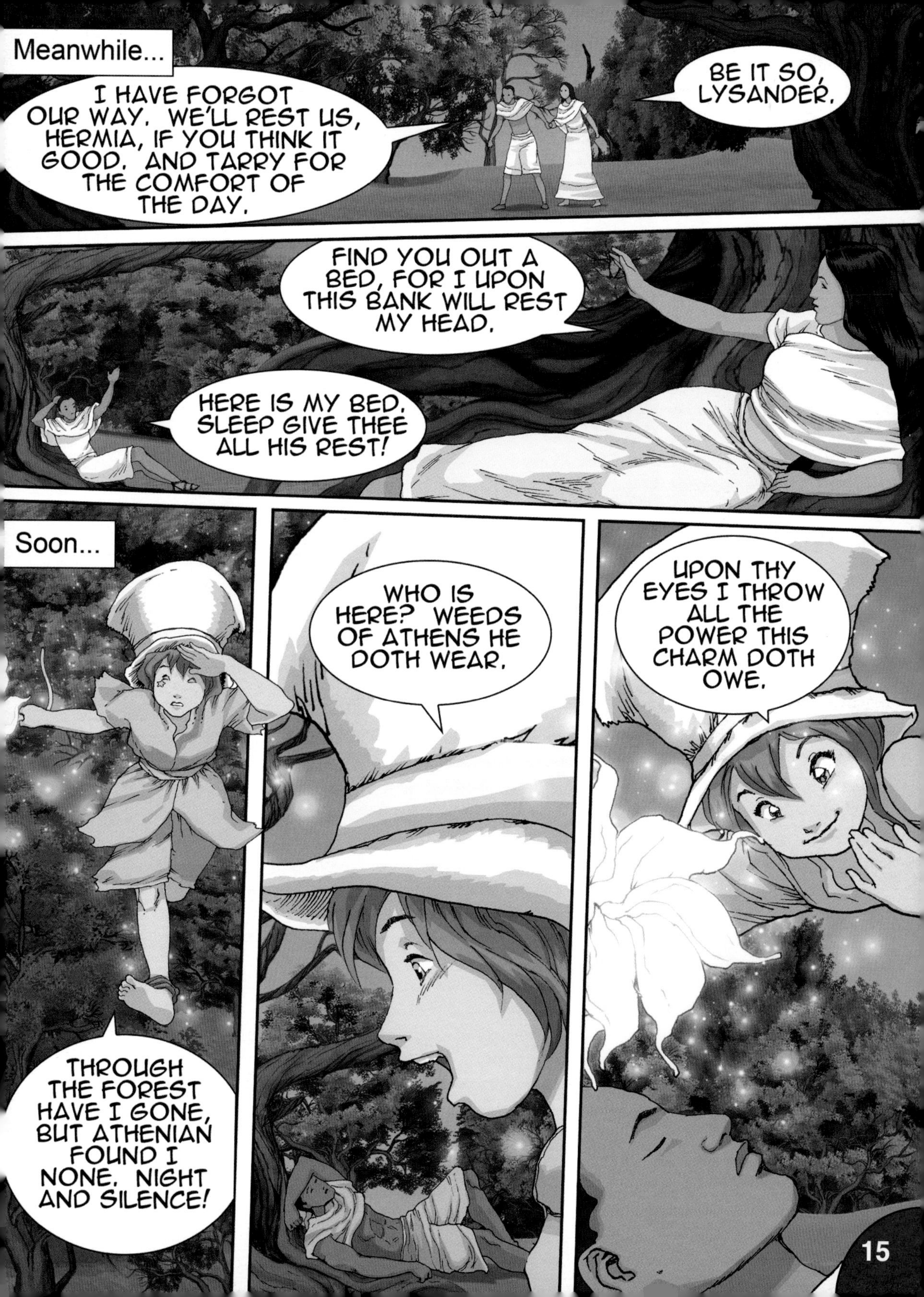

Meanwhile...
I HAVE FORGOT OUR WAY. WE'LL REST US, HERMIA, IF YOU THINK IT GOOD. AND TARRY FOR THE COMFORT OF THE DAY.
BE IT SO, LYSANDER.
FIND YOU OUT A BED, FOR I UPON THIS BANK WILL REST MY HEAD.
HERE IS MY BED. SLEEP GIVE THEE ALL HIS REST!
Soon...
THROUGH THE FOREST HAVE I GONE, BUT ATHENIAN FOUND I NONE. NIGHT AND SILENCE!
WHO IS HERE? WEEDS OF ATHENS HE DOTH WEAR.
UPON THY EYES I THROW ALL THE POWER THIS CHARM DOTH OWE.

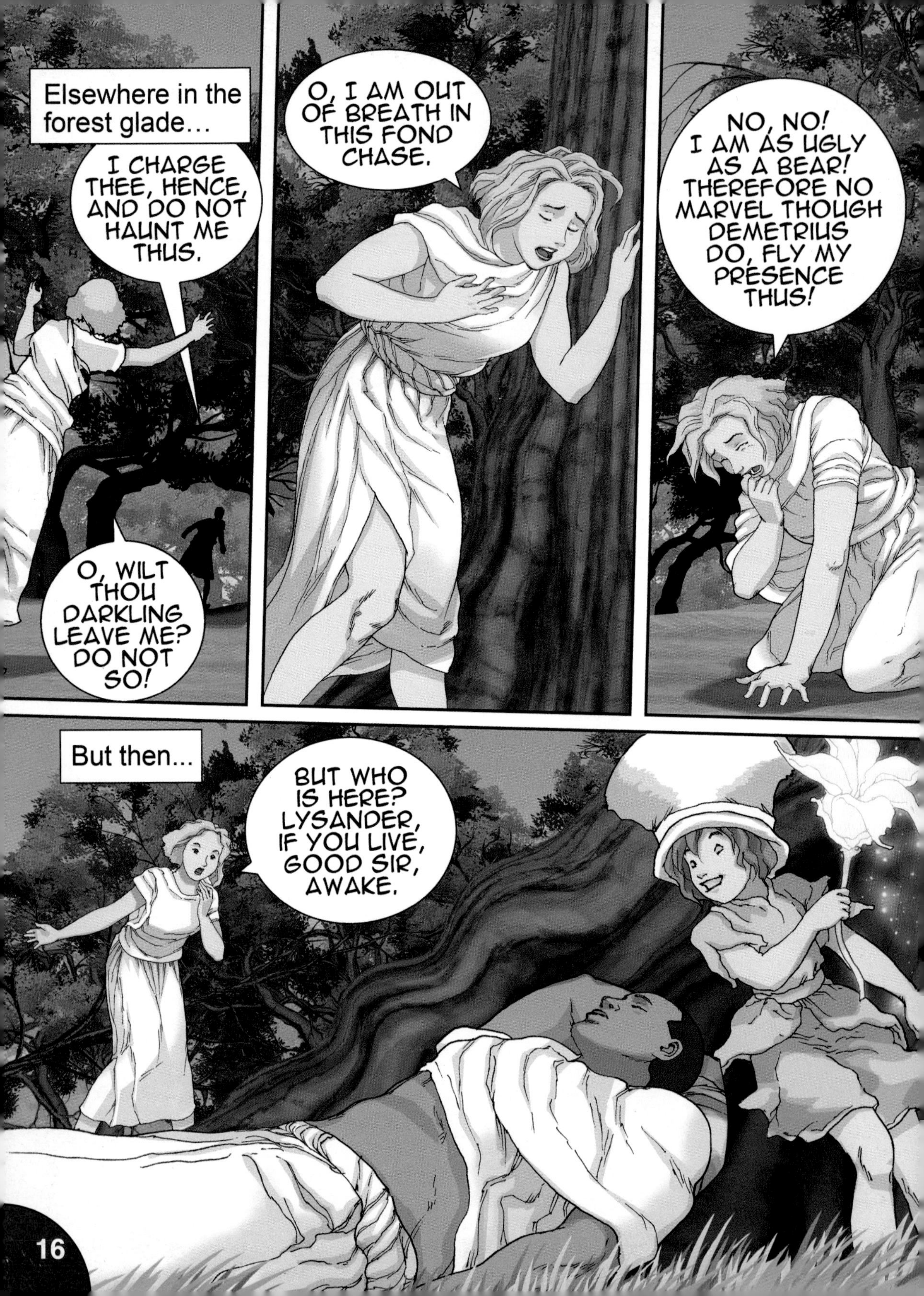
Elsewhere in the forest glade…
I CHARGE THEE, HENCE, AND DO NOT HAUNT ME THUS.
O, WILT THOU DARKLING LEAVE ME? DO NOT SO!
O, I AM OUT OF BREATH IN THIS FOND CHASE.
NO, NO! I AM AS UGLY AS A BEAR! THEREFORE NO MARVEL THOUGH DEMETRIUS DO, FLY MY PRESENCE THUS!
But then...
BUT WHO IS HERE? LYSANDER, IF YOU LIVE, GOOD SIR, AWAKE.

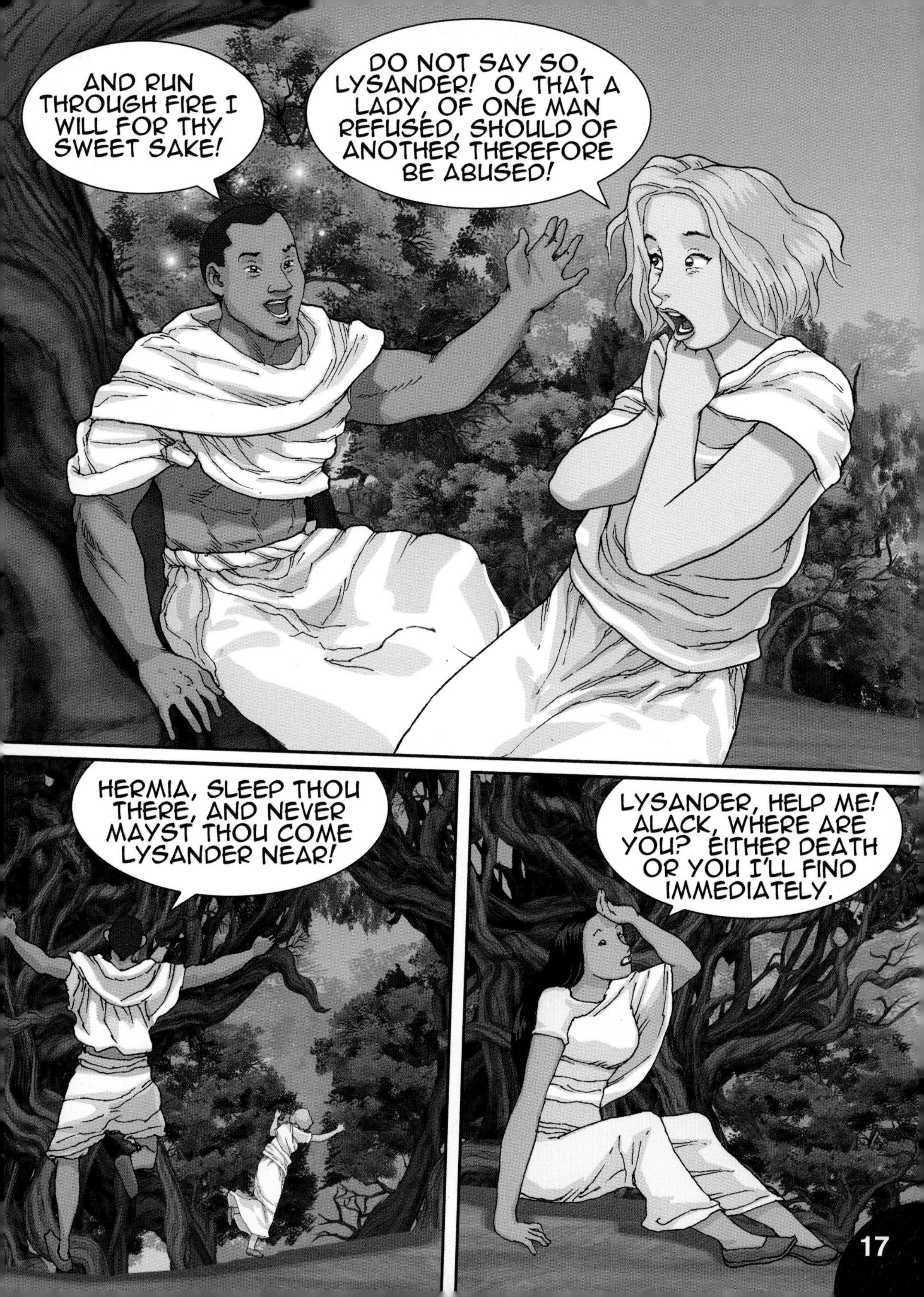
AND RUN THROUGH FIRE I WILL FOR THY SWEET SAKE!
DO NOT SAY SO, LYSANDER! O, THAT A LADY, OF ONE MAN REFUSED, SHOULD OF ANOTHER THEREFORE BE ABUSED!
HERMIA, SLEEP THOU THERE, AND NEVER MAYST THOU COME LYSANDER NEAR!
LYSANDER, HELP ME! ALACK, WHERE ARE YOU? EITHER DEATH OR YOU I'LL FIND IMMEDIATELY.

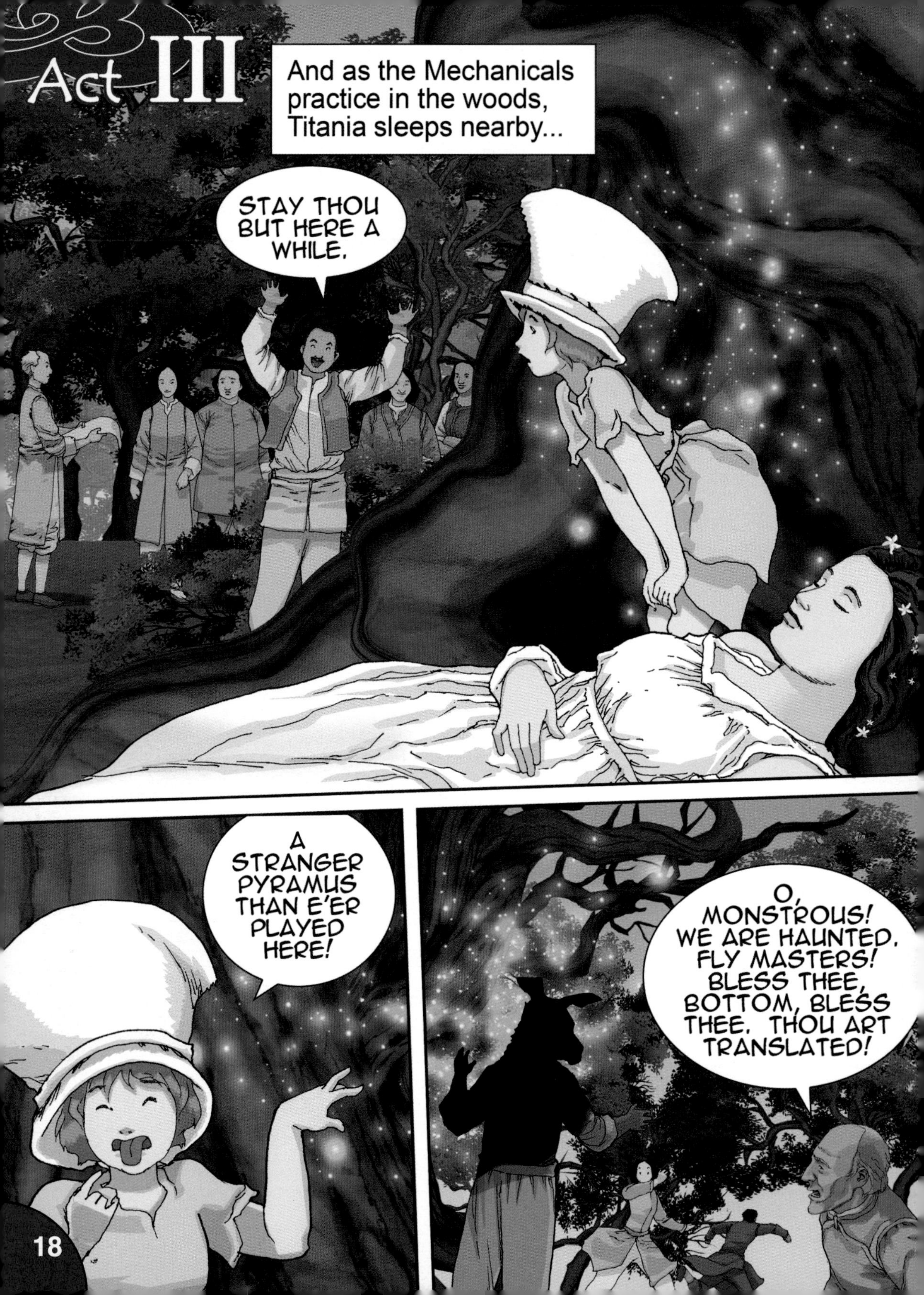
Act III
And as the Mechanicals practice in the woods, Titania sleeps nearby...
STAY THOU BUT HERE A WHILE.
A STRANGER PYRAMUS THAN E'ER PLAYED HERE!
O, MONSTROUS! WE ARE HAUNTED. FLY MASTERS! BLESS THEE, BOTTOM, BLESS THEE. THOU ART TRANSLATED!

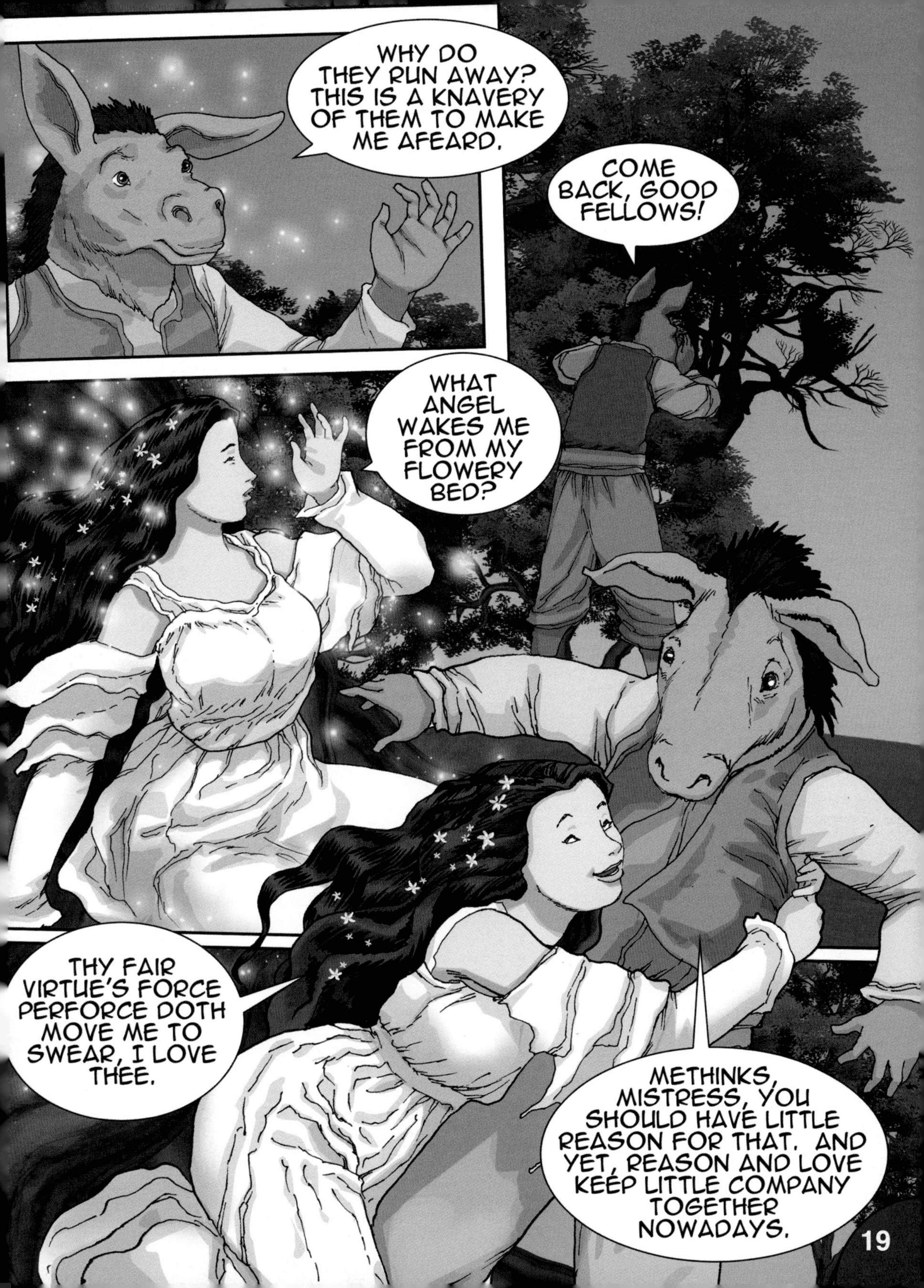
WHY DO THEY RUN AWAY? THIS IS A KNAVERY OF THEM TO MAKE ME AFEARD.
COME BACK, GOOD FELLOWS!
WHAT ANGEL WAKES ME FROM MY FLOWERY BED?
THY FAIR VIRTUE'S FORCE PERFORCE DOTH MOVE ME TO SWEAR, I LOVE THEE.
METHINKS, MISTRESS, YOU SHOULD HAVE LITTLE REASON FOR THAT. AND YET, REASON AND LOVE KEEP LITTLE COMPANY TOGETHER NOWADAYS.

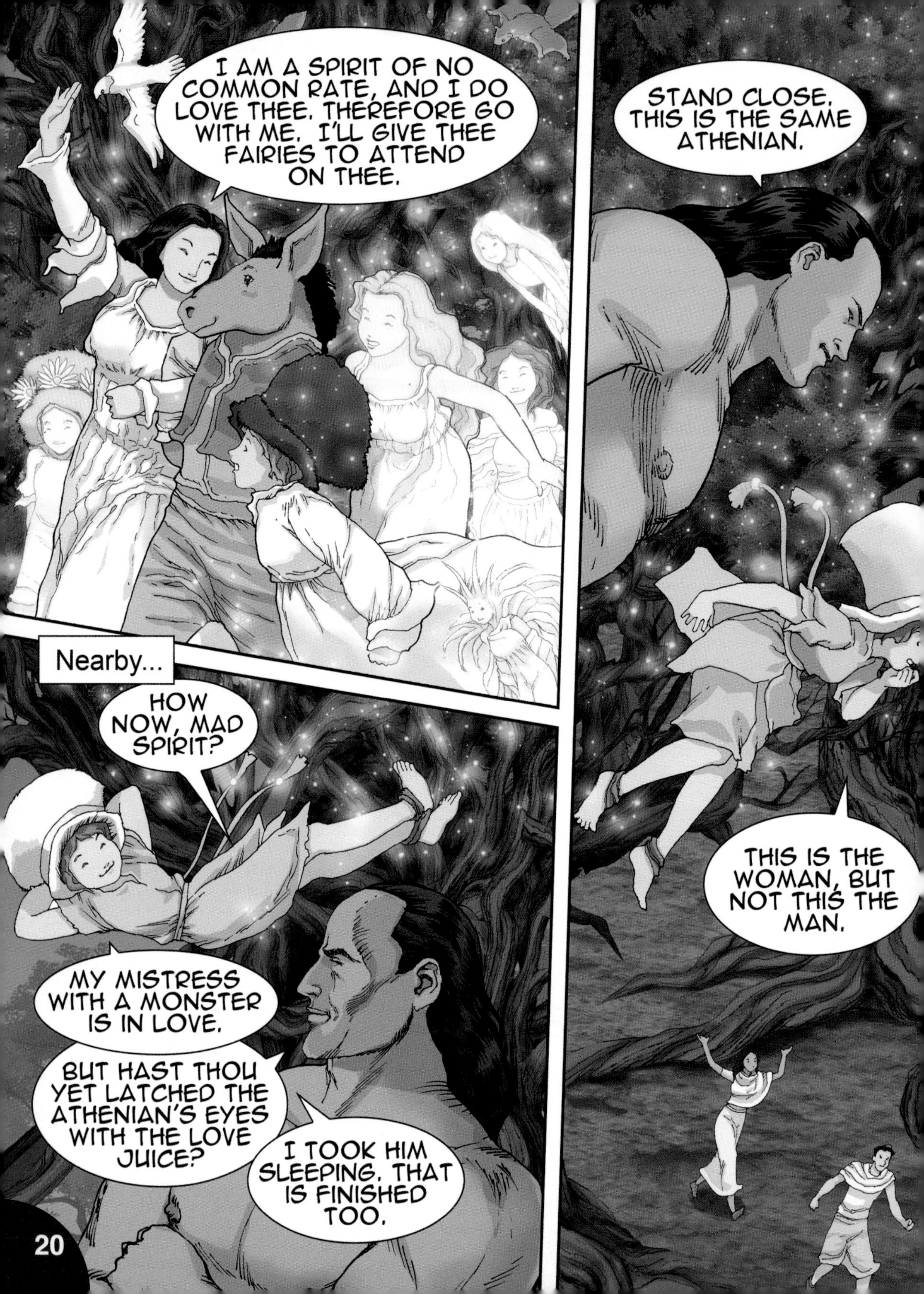
I AM A SPIRIT OF NO COMMON RATE, AND I DO LOVE THEE. THEREFORE GO WITH ME. I'LL GIVE THEE FAIRIES TO ATTEND ON THEE.
Nearby...
HOW NOW, MAD SPIRIT?
MY MISTRESS WITH A MONSTER IS IN LOVE.
BUT HAST THOU YET LATCHED THE ATHENIAN'S EYES WITH THE LOVE JUICE?
I TOOK HIM SLEEPING. THAT IS FINISHED TOO.
STAND CLOSE. THIS IS THE SAME ATHENIAN.
THIS IS THE WOMAN, BUT NOT THIS THE MAN.

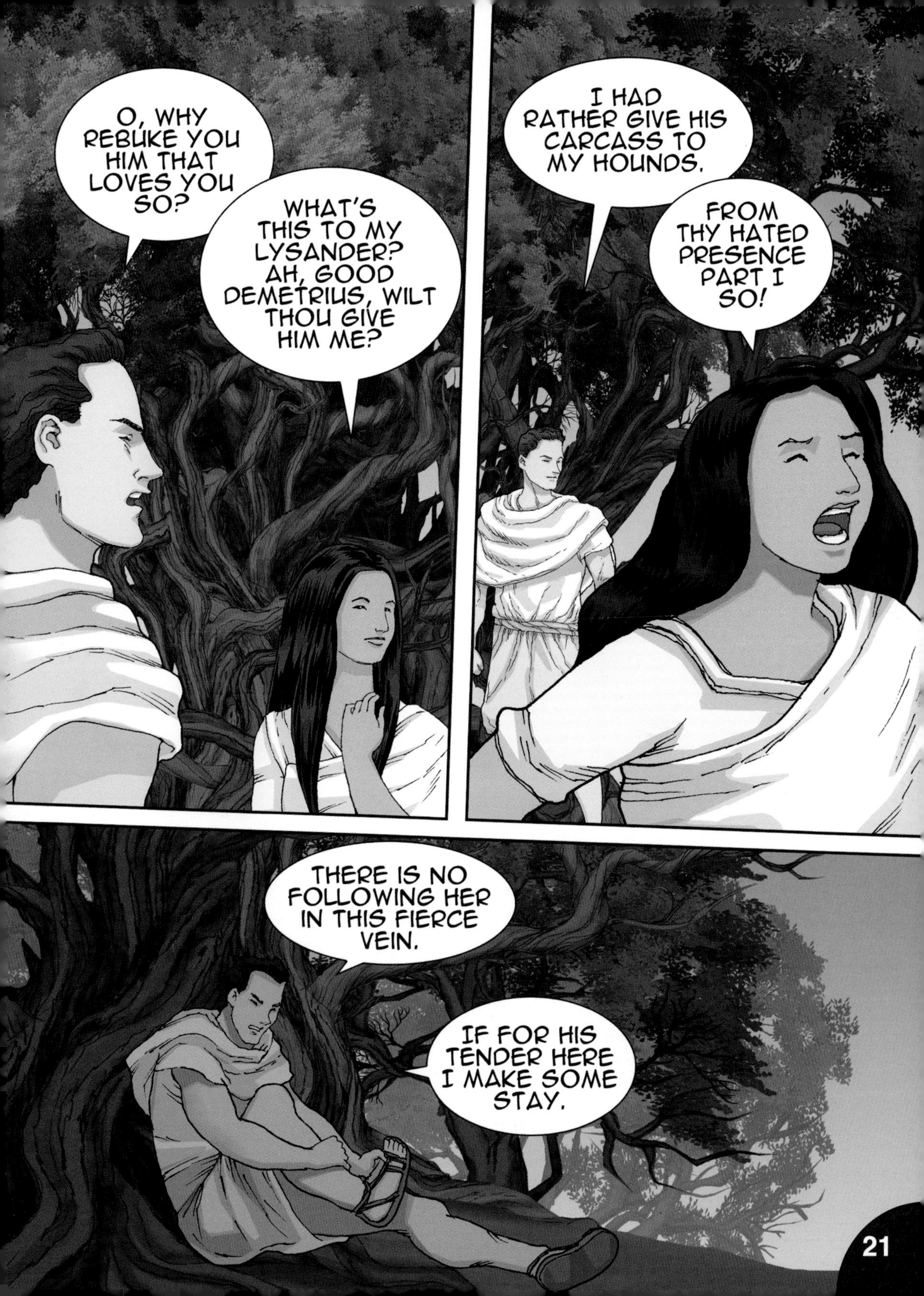
O, WHY REBUKE YOU HIM THAT LOVES YOU SO?
WHAT'S THIS TO MY LYSANDER? AH, GOOD DEMETRIUS, WILT THOU GIVE HIM ME?
I HAD RATHER GIVE HIS CARCASS TO MY HOUNDS.
FROM THY HATED PRESENCE PART I SO!
THERE IS NO FOLLOWING HER IN THIS FIERCE VEIN.
IF FOR HIS TENDER HERE I MAKE SOME STAY.

THOU HAST MISTAKEN QUITE! ABOUT THE WOOD GO SWIFTER THAN THE WIND, AND HELENA OF ATHENS LOOK THOU FIND.
I GO, I GO! LOOK HOW I GO!
WHEN HIS LOVE HE DOTH ESPY, LET HER SHINE. WHEN THOU WAKEST, IF SHE BE BY, BEG OF HER FOR REMEDY.

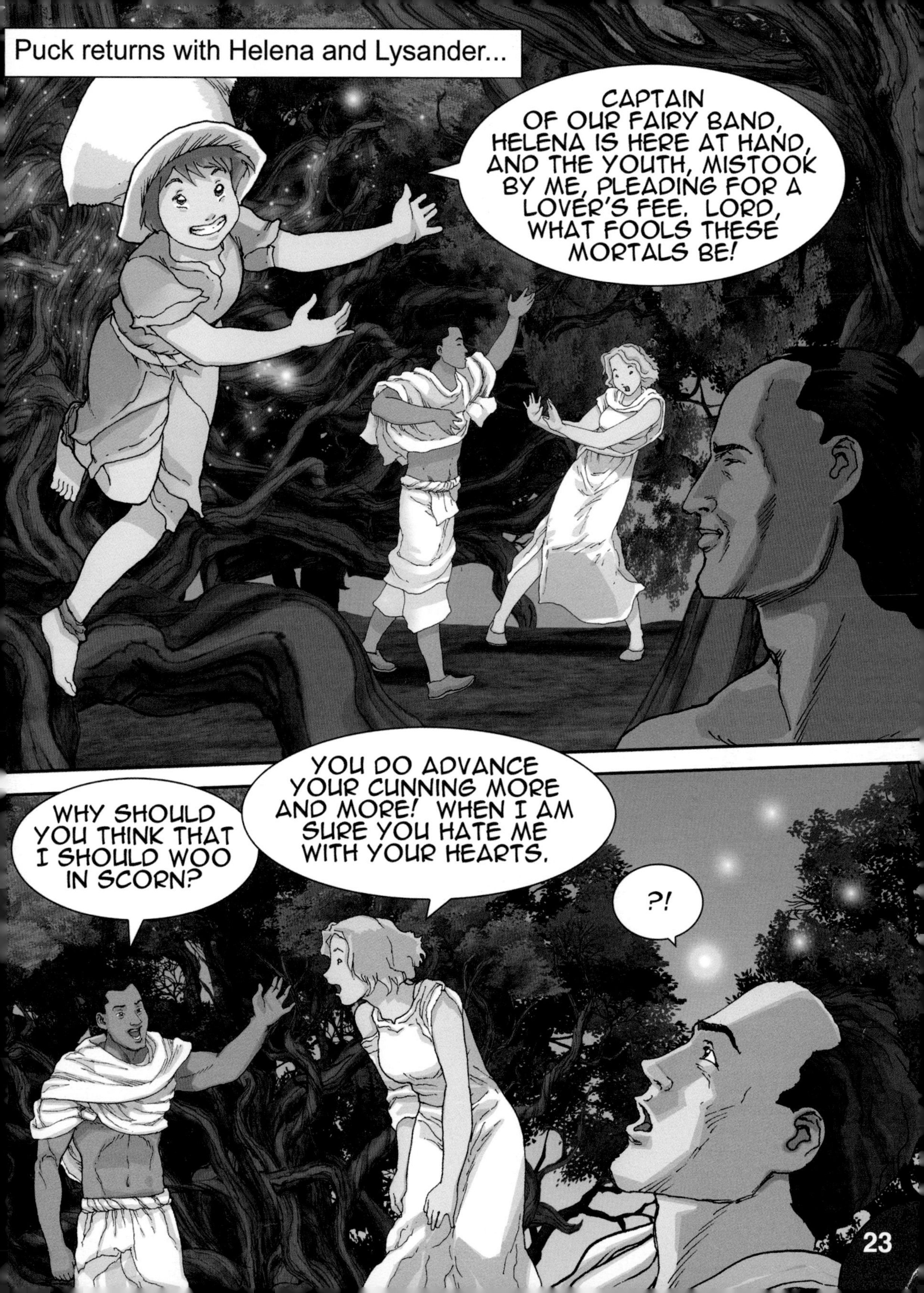
Puck returns with Helena and Lysander...
CAPTAIN OF OUR FAIRY BAND, HELENA IS HERE AT HAND, AND THE YOUTH, MISTOOK BY ME, PLEADING FOR A LOVER'S FEE. LORD, WHAT FOOLS THESE MORTALS BE!
WHY SHOULD YOU THINK THAT I SHOULD WOO IN SCORN?
YOU DO ADVANCE YOUR CUNNING MORE AND MORE! WHEN I AM SURE YOU HATE ME WITH YOUR HEARTS.
?!

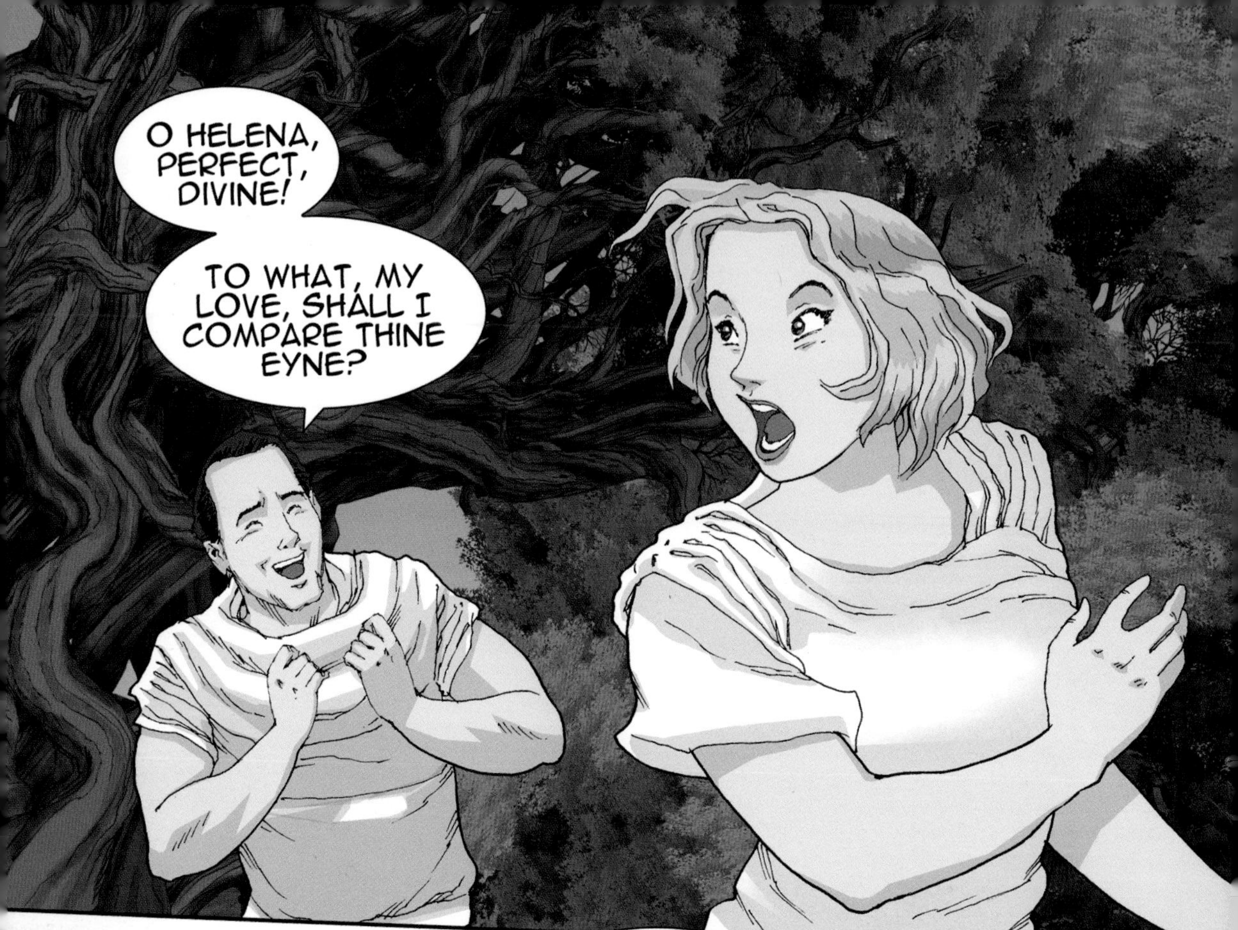
O HELENA, PERFECT, DIVINE!
TO WHAT, MY LOVE, SHALL I COMPARE THINE EYNE?

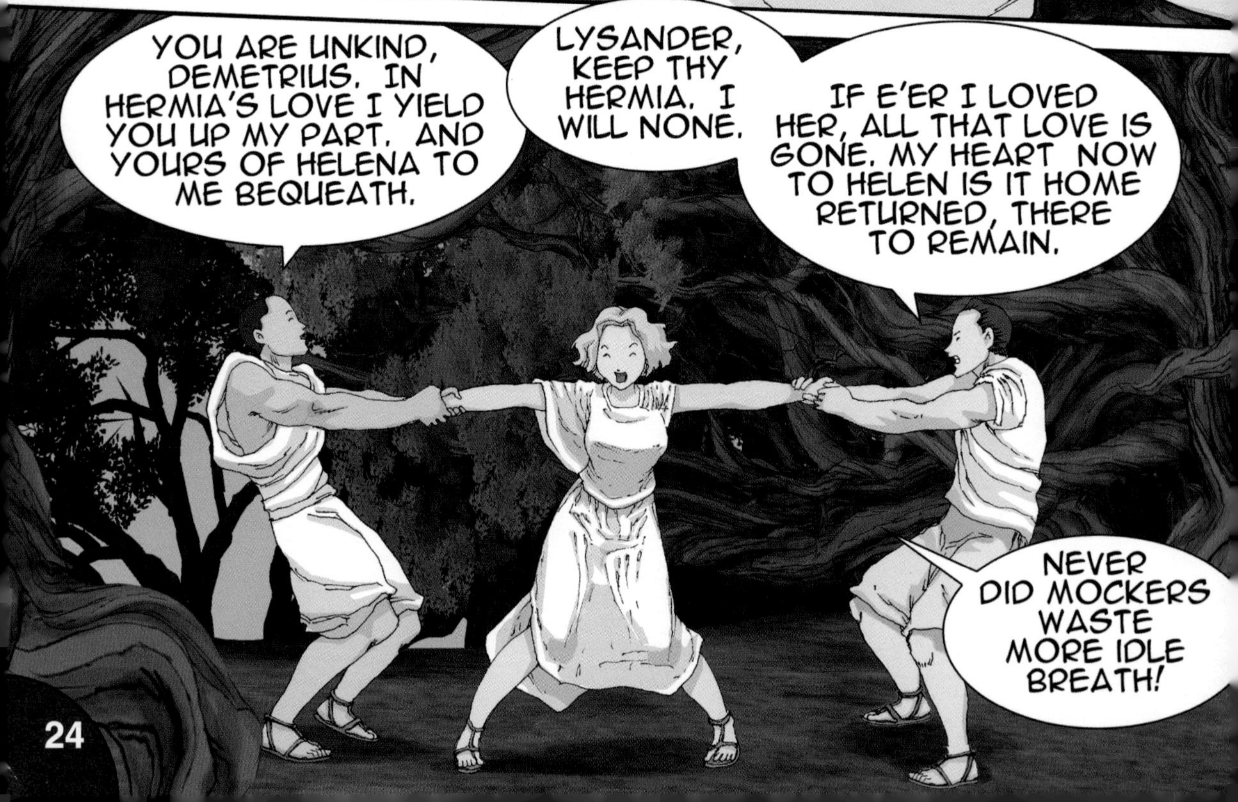
YOU ARE UNKIND, DEMETRIUS. IN HERMIA'S LOVE I YIELD YOU UP MY PART. AND YOURS OF HELENA TO ME BEQUEATH.
LYSANDER, KEEP THY HERMIA. I WILL NONE.
IF E'ER I LOVED HER, ALL THAT LOVE IS GONE. MY HEART NOW TO HELEN IS IT HOME RETURNED, THERE TO REMAIN.
NEVER DID MOCKERS WASTE MORE IDLE BREATH!

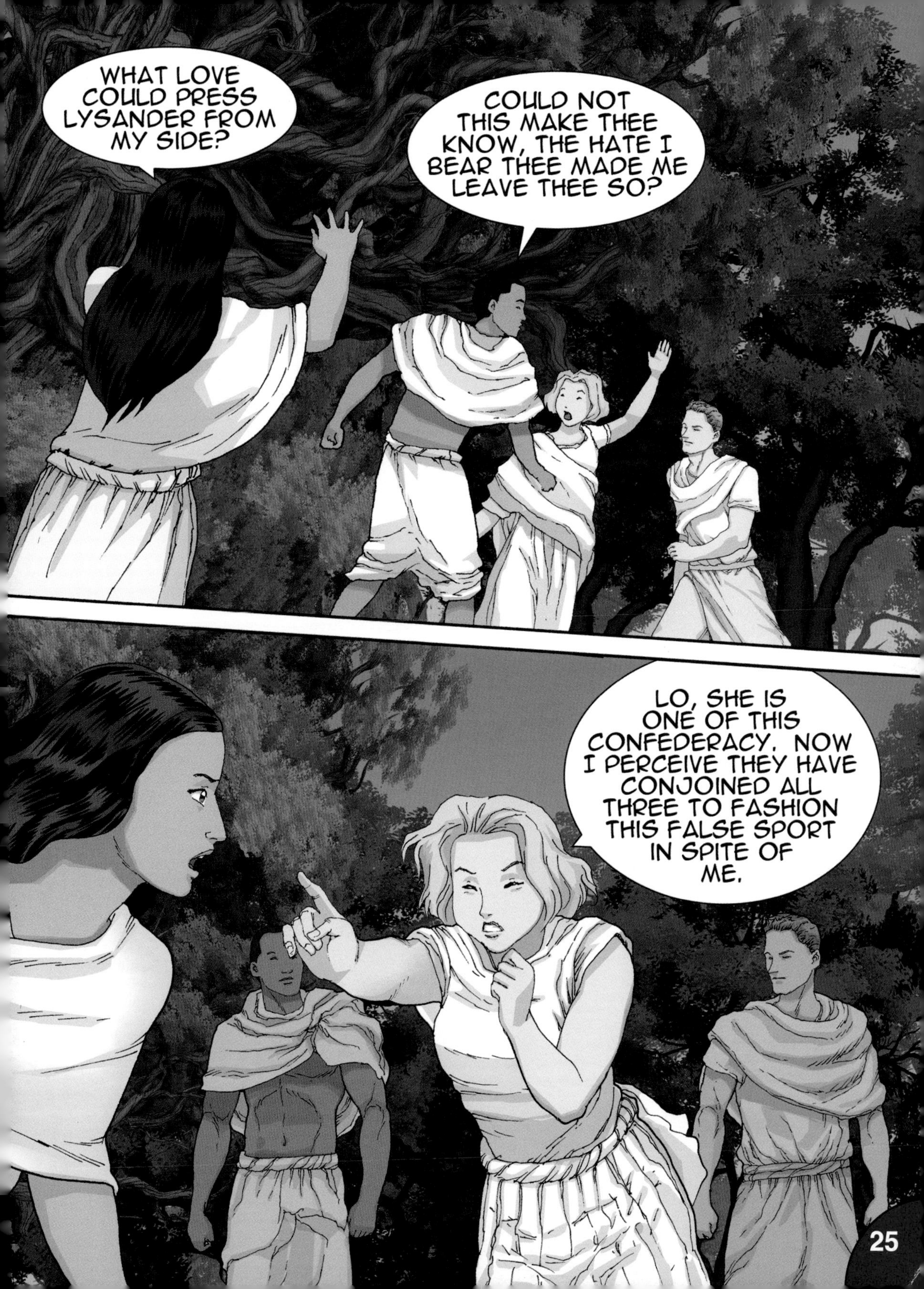

WHAT LOVE COULD PRESS LYSANDER FROM MY SIDE?
COULD NOT THIS MAKE THEE KNOW, THE HATE I BEAR THEE MADE ME LEAVE THEE SO?
LO, SHE IS ONE OF THIS CONFEDERACY. NOW I PERCEIVE THEY HAVE CONJOINED ALL THREE TO FASHION THIS FALSE SPORT IN SPITE OF ME.

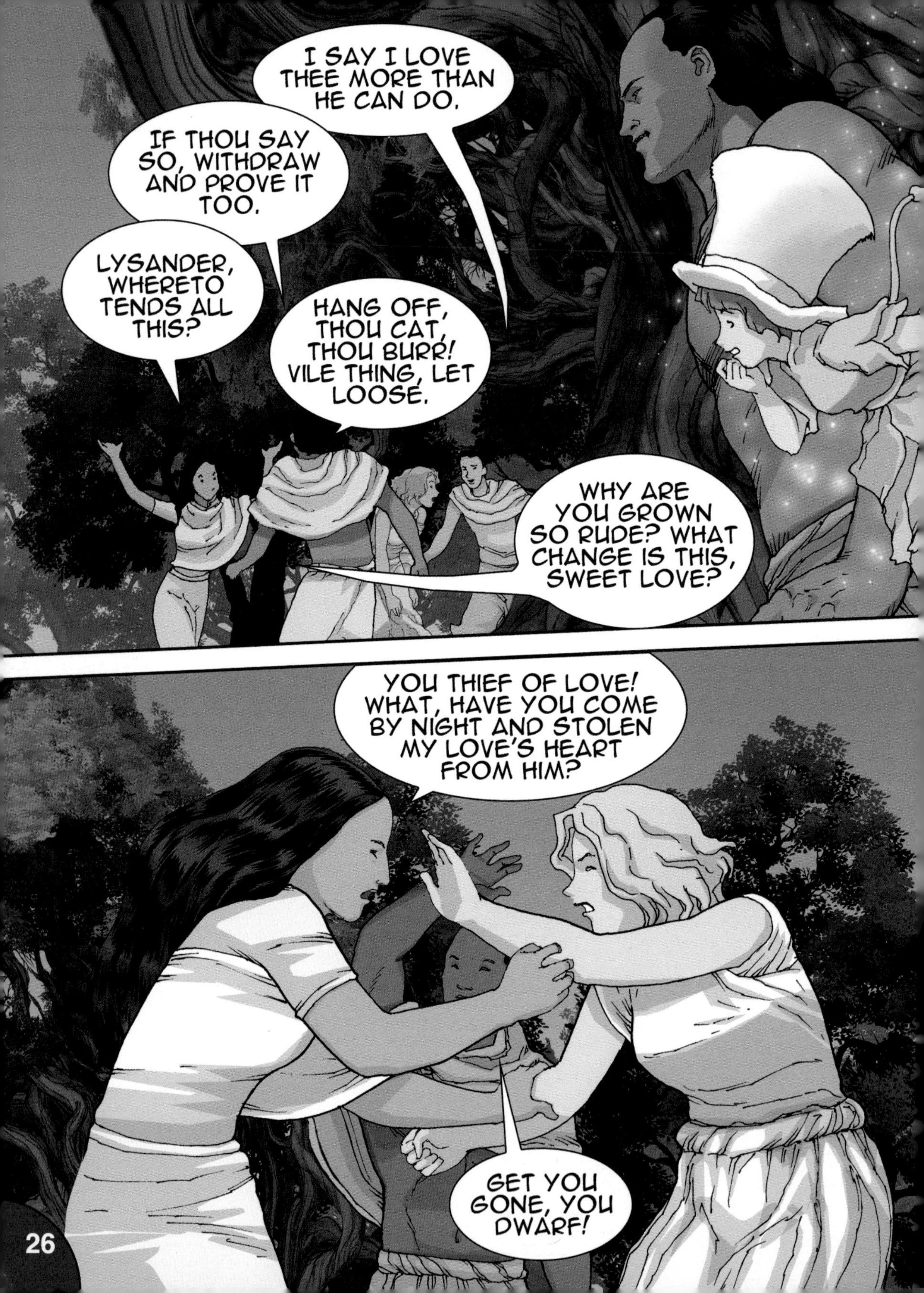

I SAY I LOVE THEE MORE THAN HE CAN DO.
IF THOU SAY SO, WITHDRAW AND PROVE IT TOO.
LYSANDER, WHERETO TENDS ALL THIS?
HANG OFF, THOU CAT, THOU BURR! VILE THING, LET LOOSE.
WHY ARE YOU GROWN SO RUDE? WHAT CHANGE IS THIS, SWEET LOVE?
YOU THIEF OF LOVE! WHAT, HAVE YOU COME BY NIGHT AND STOLEN MY LOVE'S HEART FROM HIM?
GET YOU GONE, YOU DWARF!

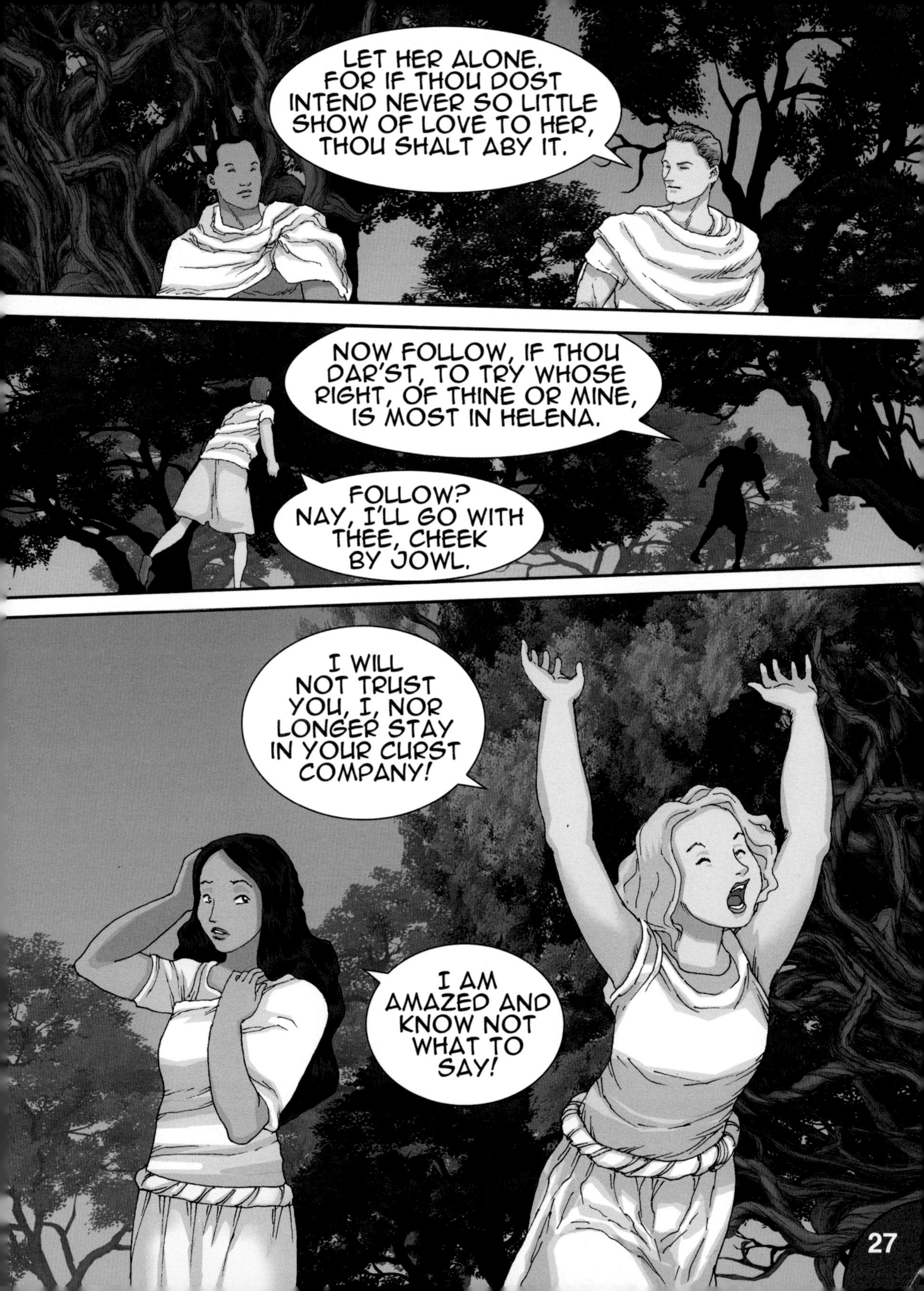
LET HER ALONE. FOR IF THOU DOST INTEND NEVER SO LITTLE SHOW OF LOVE TO HER, THOU SHALT ABY IT.
NOW FOLLOW, IF THOU DAR'ST, TO TRY WHOSE RIGHT, OF THINE OR MINE, IS MOST IN HELENA.
FOLLOW? NAY, I'LL GO WITH THEE, CHEEK BY JOWL.
I WILL NOT TRUST YOU, I, NOR LONGER STAY IN YOUR CURST COMPANY!
I AM AMAZED AND KNOW NOT WHAT TO SAY!

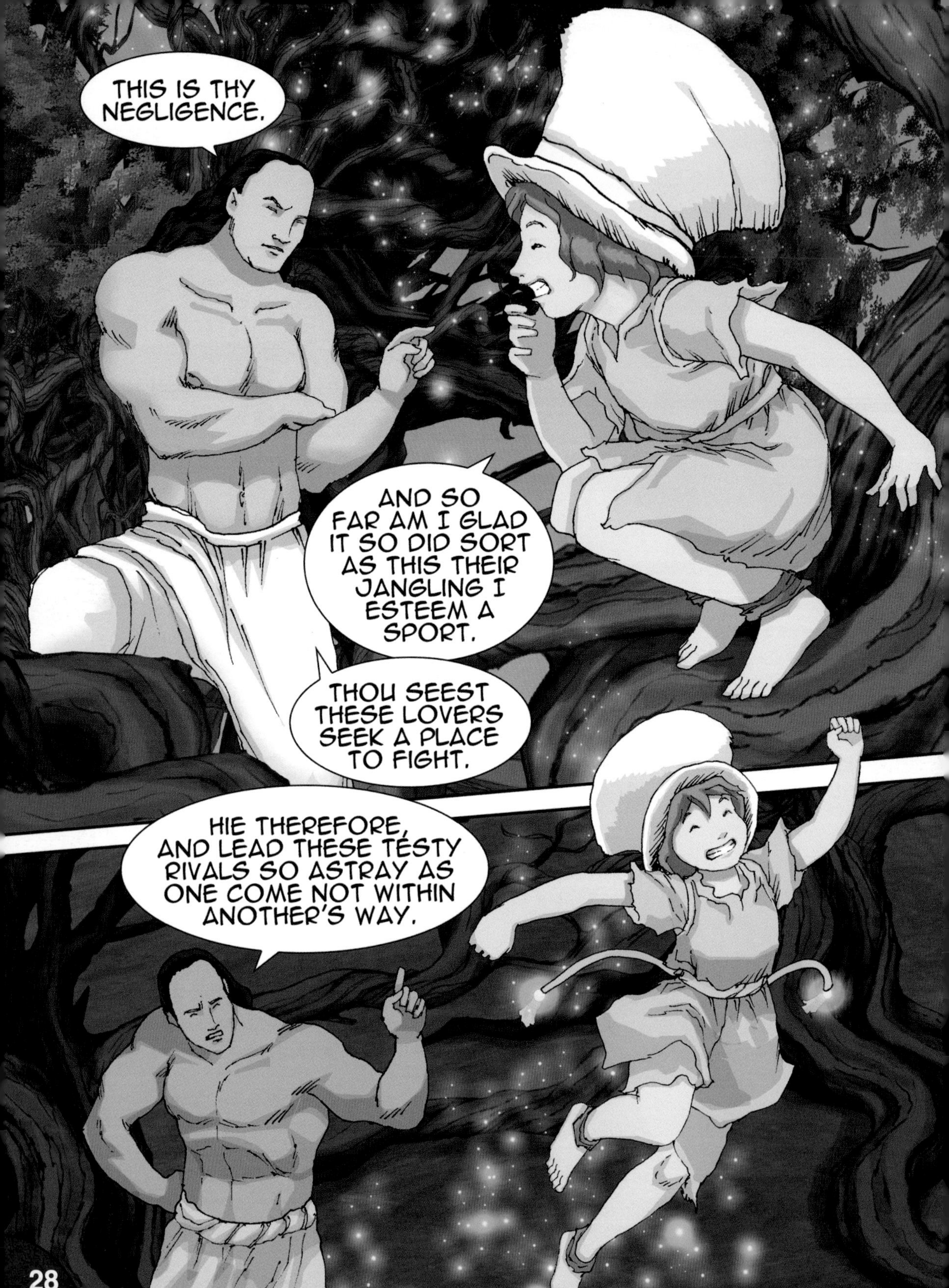
THIS IS THY NEGLIGENCE.
AND SO FAR AM I GLAD IT SO DID SORT AS THIS THEIR JANGLING I ESTEEM A SPORT.
THOU SEEST THESE LOVERS SEEK A PLACE TO FIGHT.
HIE THEREFORE, AND LEAD THESE TESTY RIVALS SO ASTRAY AS ONE COME NOT WITHIN ANOTHER'S WAY.

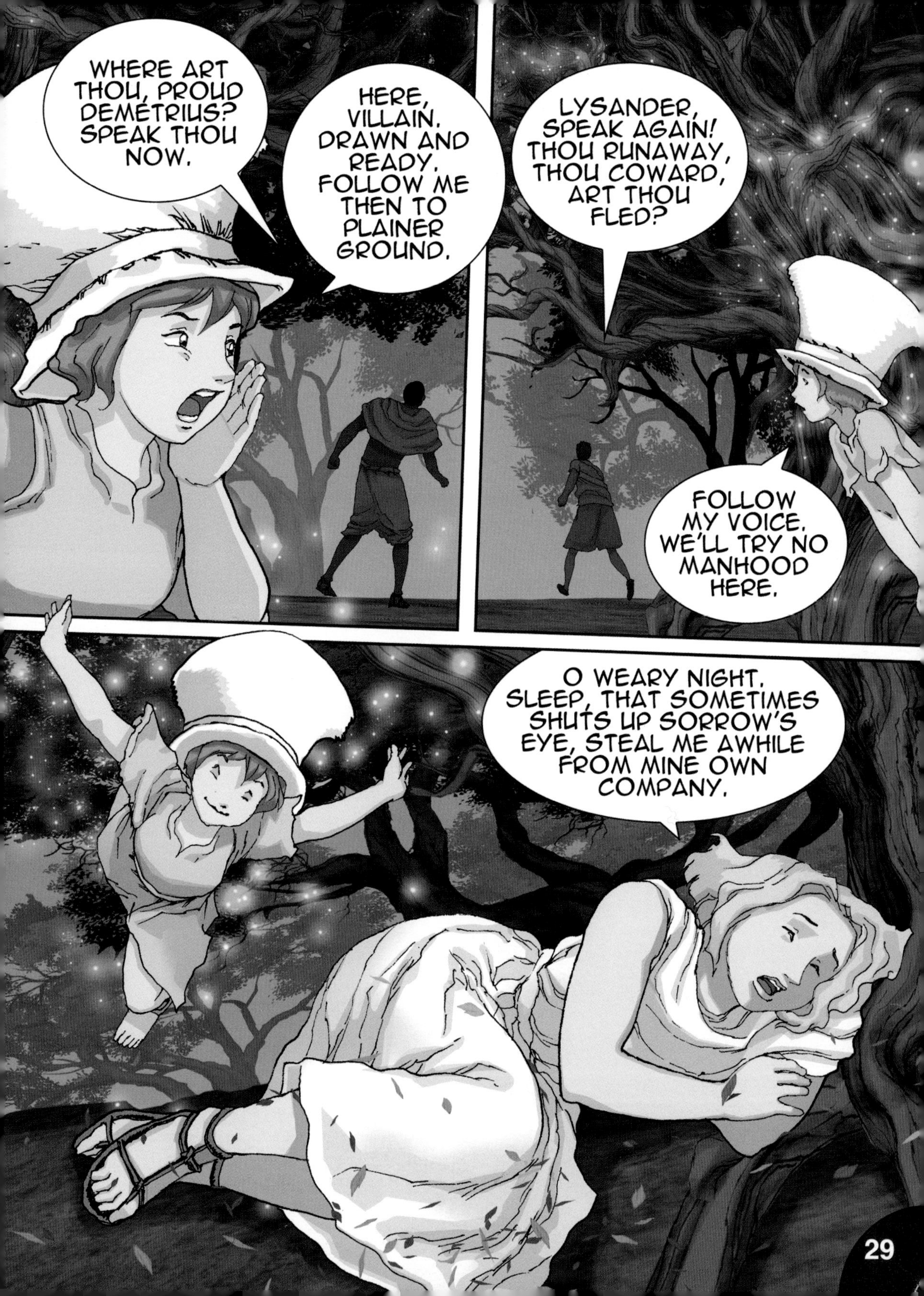

WHERE ART THOU, PROUD DEMETRIUS? SPEAK THOU NOW.
HERE, VILLAIN. DRAWN AND READY. FOLLOW ME THEN TO PLAINER GROUND.
LYSANDER, SPEAK AGAIN! THOU RUNAWAY, THOU COWARD, ART THOU FLED?
FOLLOW MY VOICE. WE'LL TRY NO MANHOOD HERE.
O WEARY NIGHT. SLEEP, THAT SOMETIMES SHUTS UP SORROW'S EYE, STEAL ME AWHILE FROM MINE OWN COMPANY.

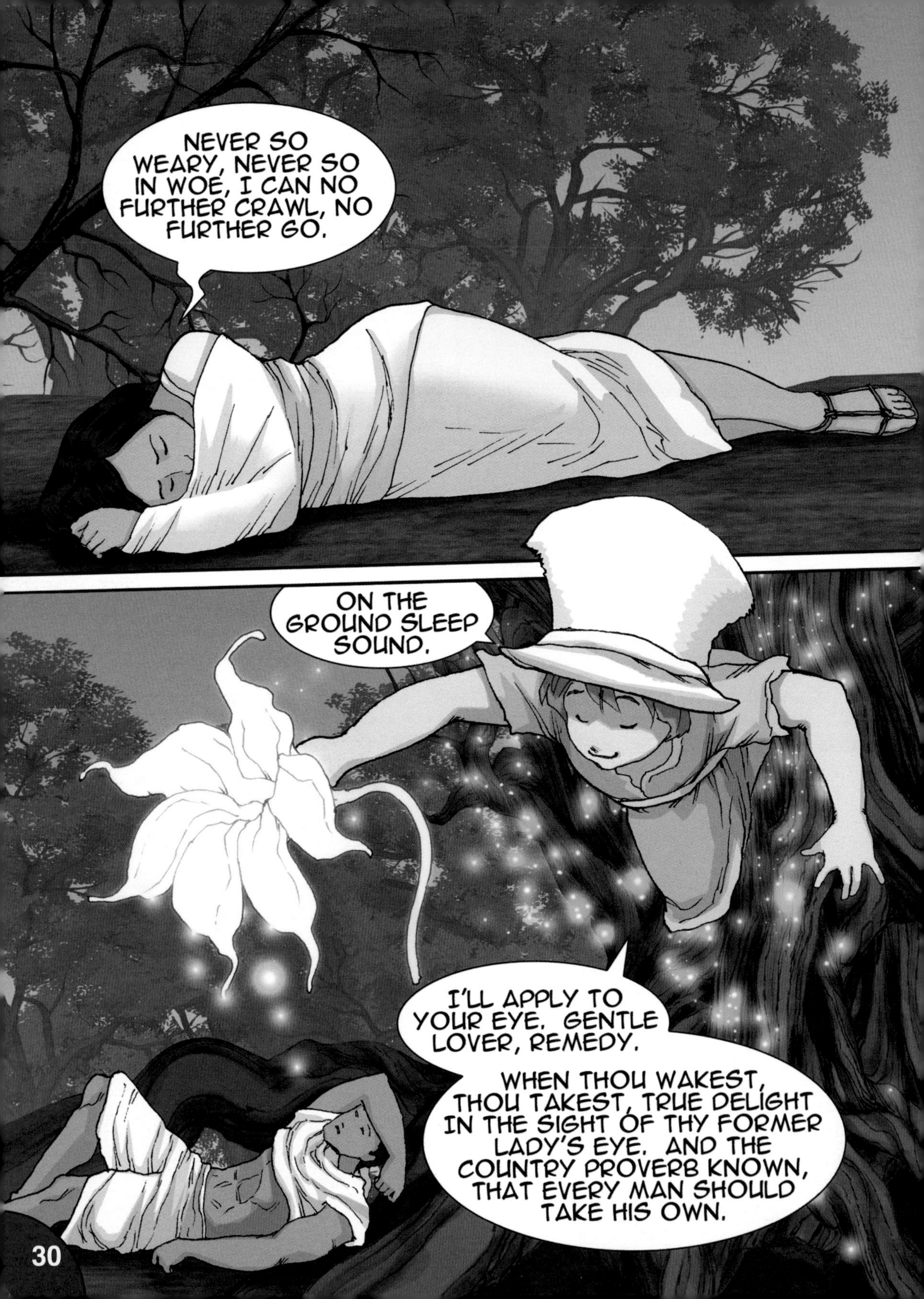
NEVER SO WEARY, NEVER SO IN WOE, I CAN NO FURTHER CRAWL, NO FURTHER GO.
ON THE GROUND SLEEP SOUND.
I'LL APPLY TO YOUR EYE. GENTLE LOVER, REMEDY.
WHEN THOU WAKEST, THOU TAKEST, TRUE DELIGHT IN THE SIGHT OF THY FORMER LADY'S EYE. AND THE COUNTRY PROVERB KNOWN, THAT EVERY MAN SHOULD TAKE HIS OWN.

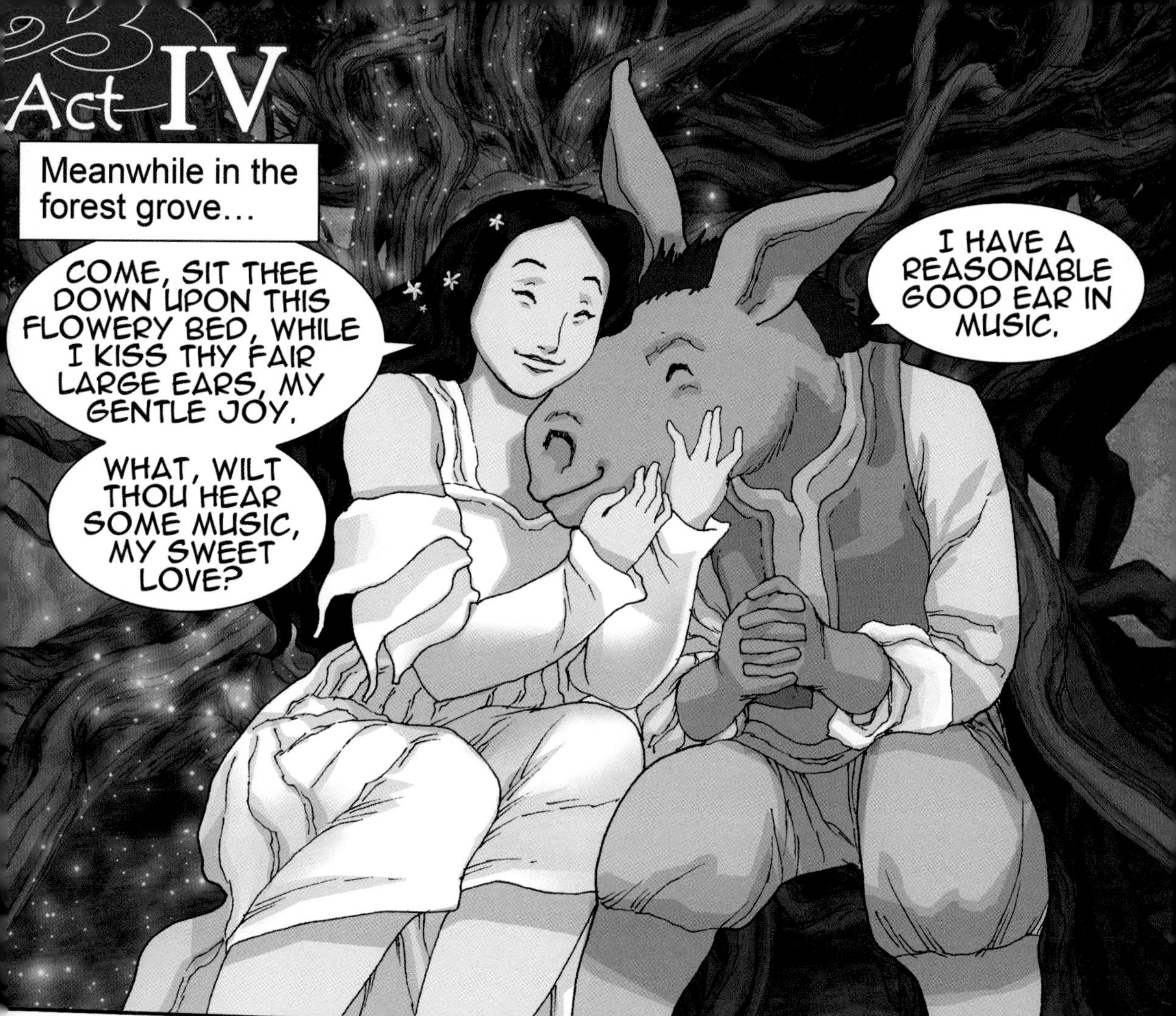
Act IV
Meanwhile in the forest grove…
COME, SIT THEE DOWN UPON THIS FLOWERY BED, WHILE I KISS THY FAIR LARGE EARS, MY GENTLE JOY.
WHAT, WILT THOU HEAR SOME MUSIC, MY SWEET LOVE?
I HAVE A REASONABLE GOOD EAR IN MUSIC.

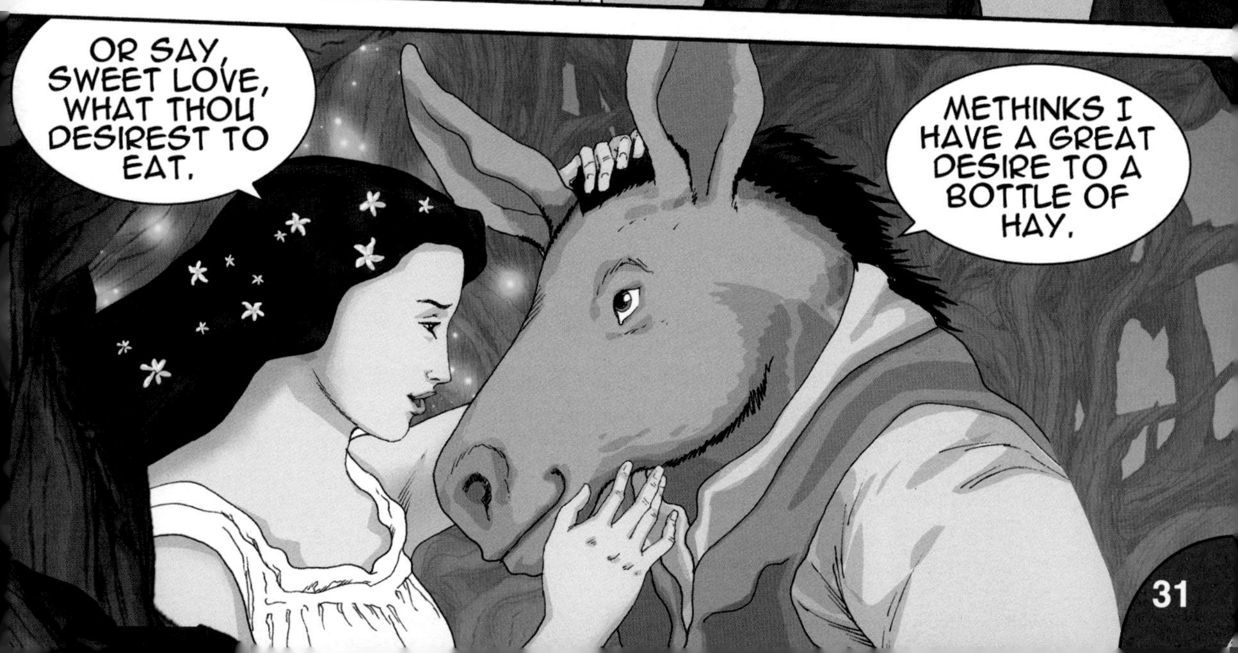
OR SAY, SWEET LOVE, WHAT THOU DESIREST TO EAT.
METHINKS I HAVE A GREAT DESIRE TO A BOTTLE OF HAY.

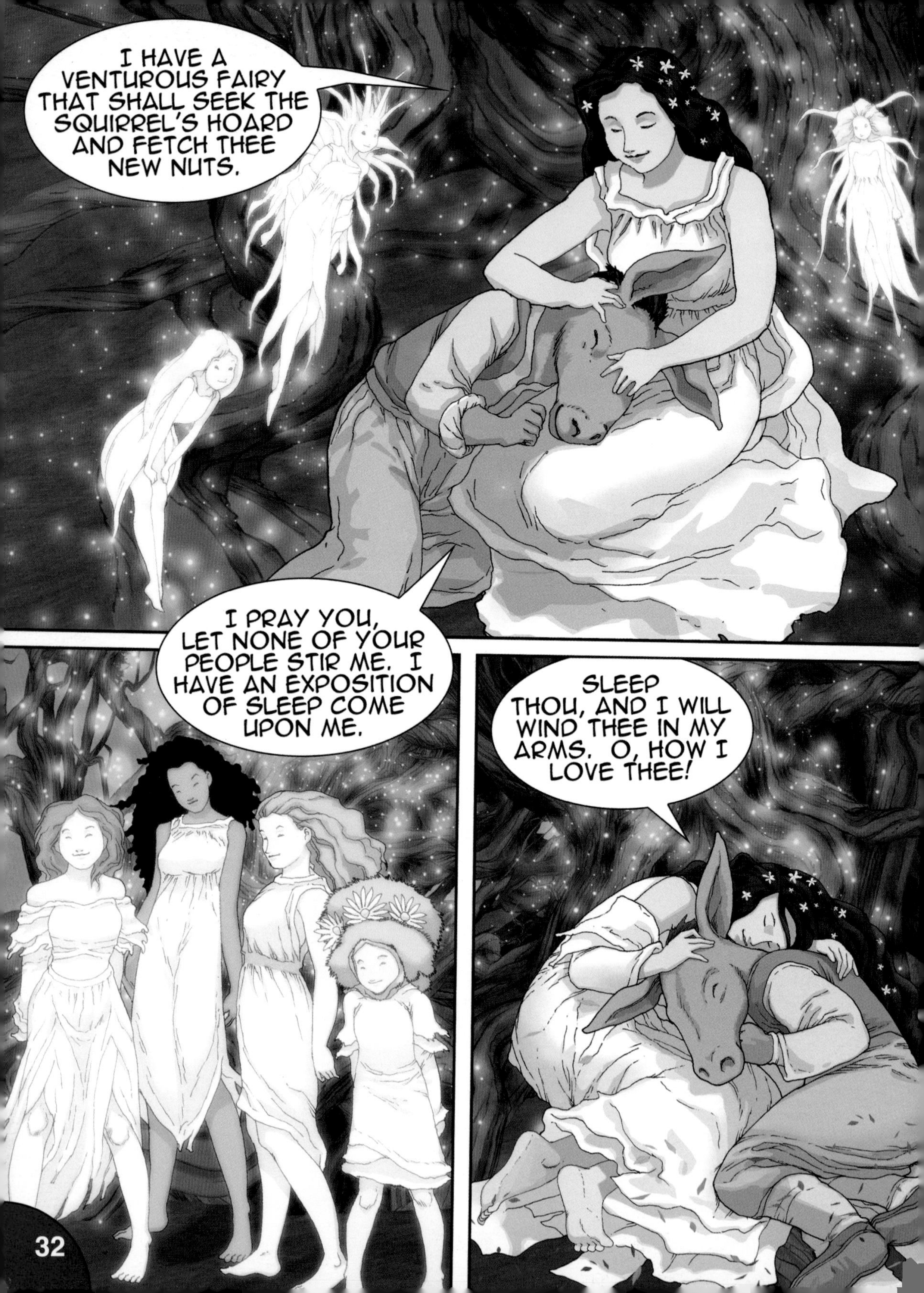
I HAVE A VENTUROUS FAIRY THAT SHALL SEEK THE SQUIRREL'S HOARD AND FETCH THEE NEW NUTS.
I PRAY YOU, LET NONE OF YOUR PEOPLE STIR ME. I HAVE AN EXPOSITION OF SLEEP COME UPON ME.
SLEEP THOU, AND I WILL WIND THEE IN MY ARMS. O, HOW I LOVE THEE!

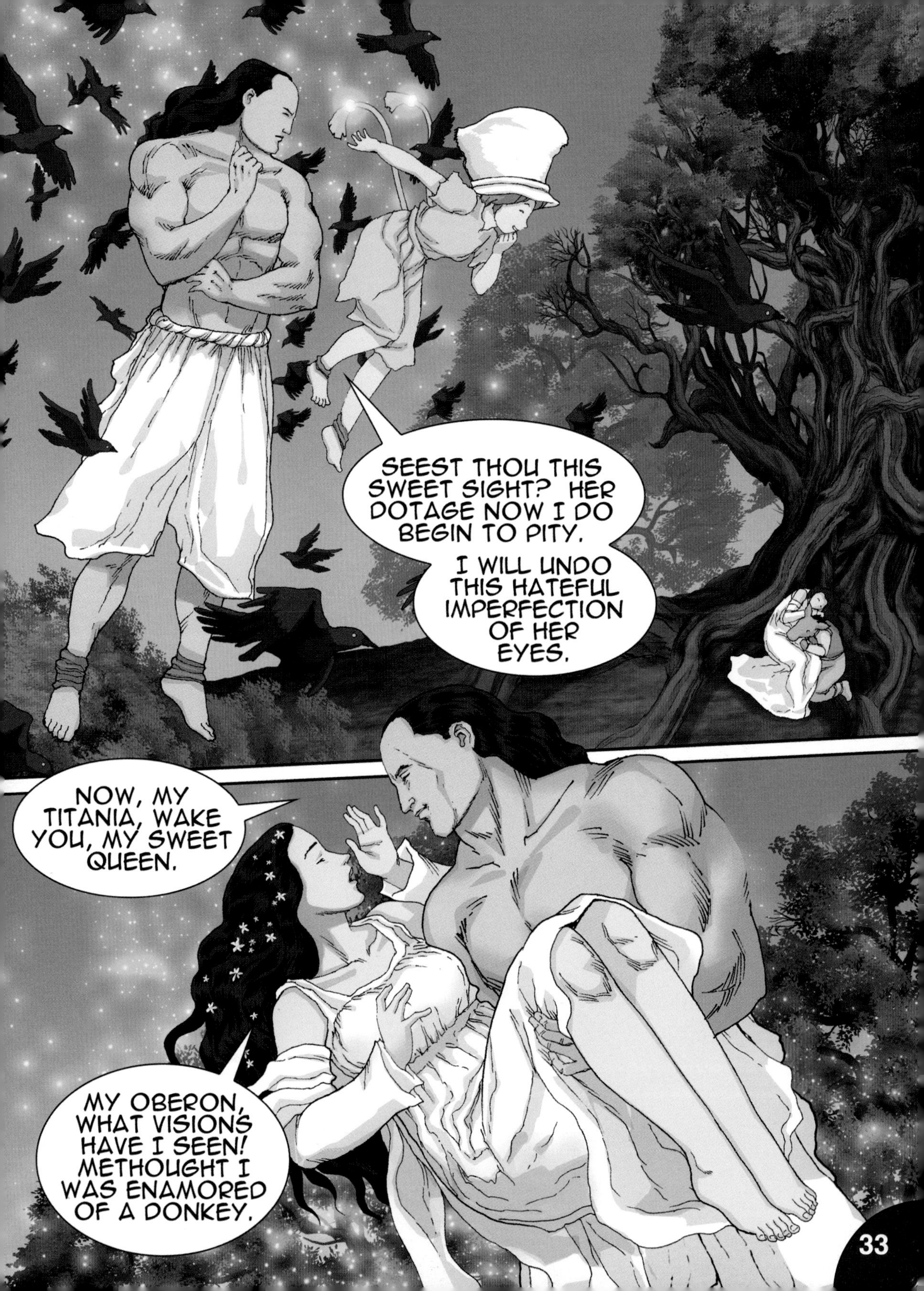
SEEST THOU THIS SWEET SIGHT? HER DOTAGE NOW I DO BEGIN TO PITY.
I WILL UNDO THIS HATEFUL IMPERFECTION OF HER EYES.
NOW, MY TITANIA, WAKE YOU, MY SWEET QUEEN.
MY OBERON, WHAT VISIONS HAVE I SEEN! METHOUGHT I WAS ENAMORED OF A DONKEY.

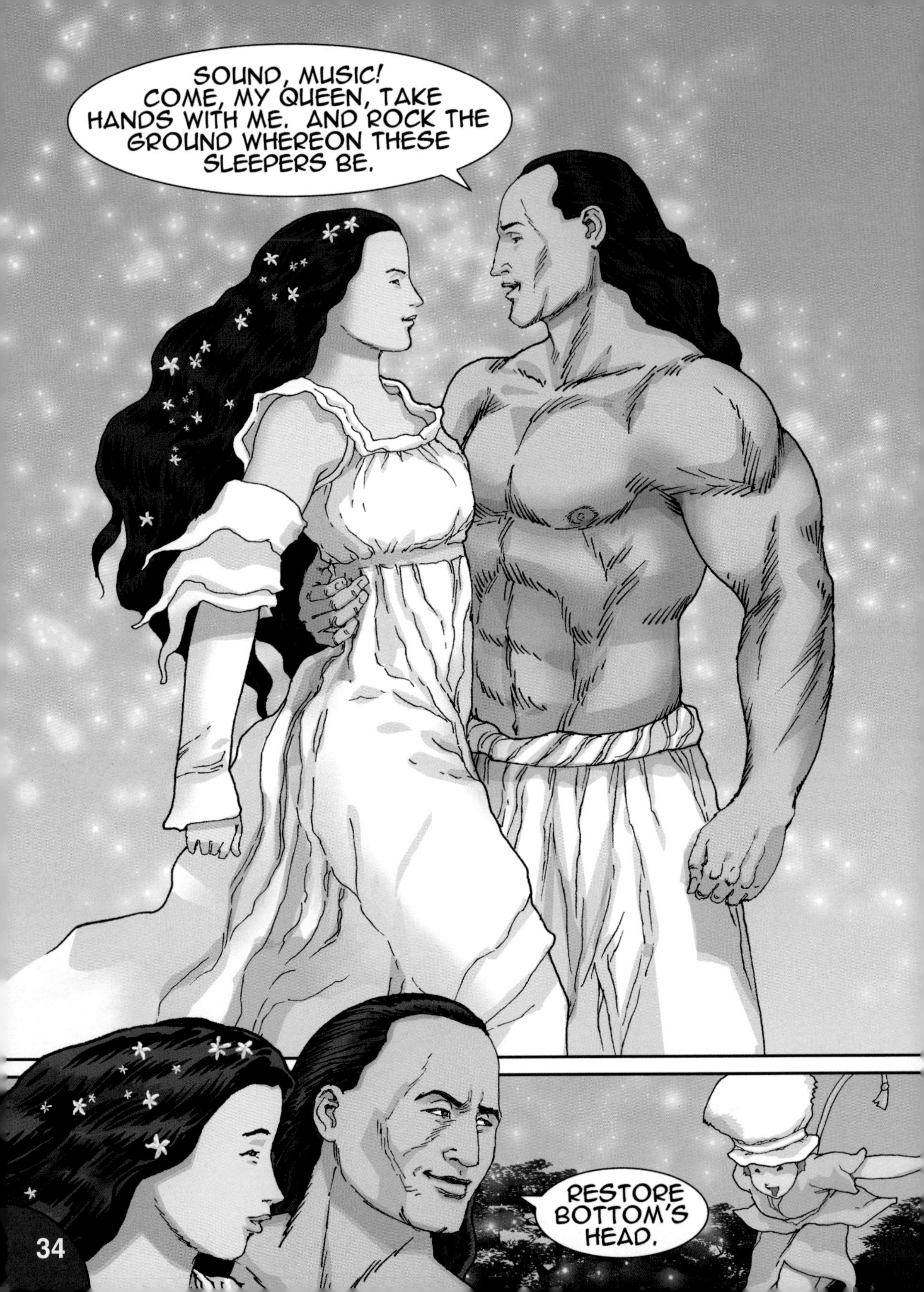
SOUND, MUSIC! COME, MY QUEEN, TAKE HANDS WITH ME. AND ROCK THE GROUND WHEREON THESE SLEEPERS BE.
RESTORE BOTTOM'S HEAD.

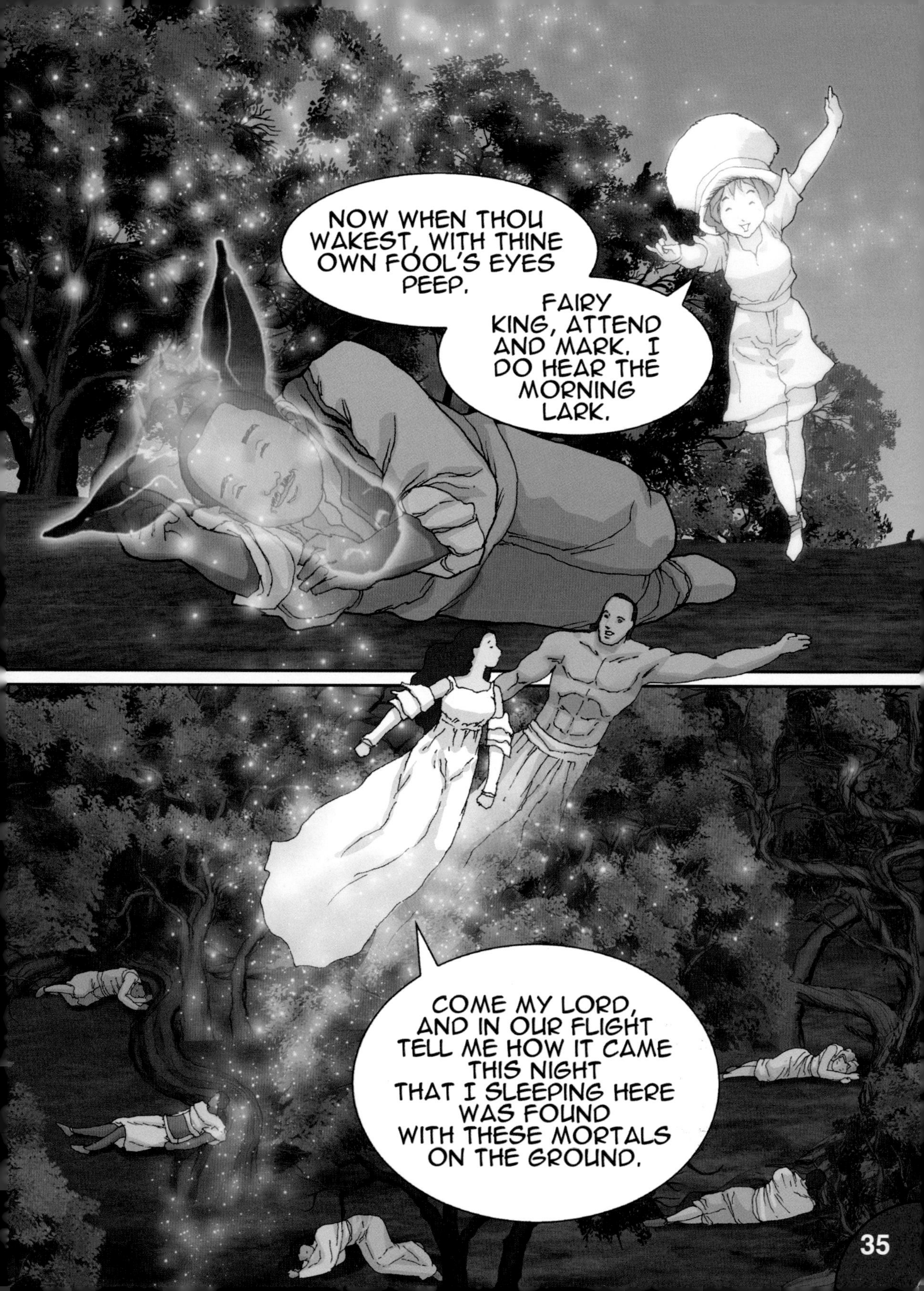
NOW WHEN THOU WAKEST, WITH THINE OWN FOOL'S EYES PEEP.
FAIRY KING, ATTEND AND MARK. I DO HEAR THE MORNING LARK.
COME MY LORD, AND IN OUR FLIGHT TELL ME HOW IT CAME THIS NIGHT THAT I SLEEPING HERE WAS FOUND WITH THESE MORTALS ON THE GROUND.

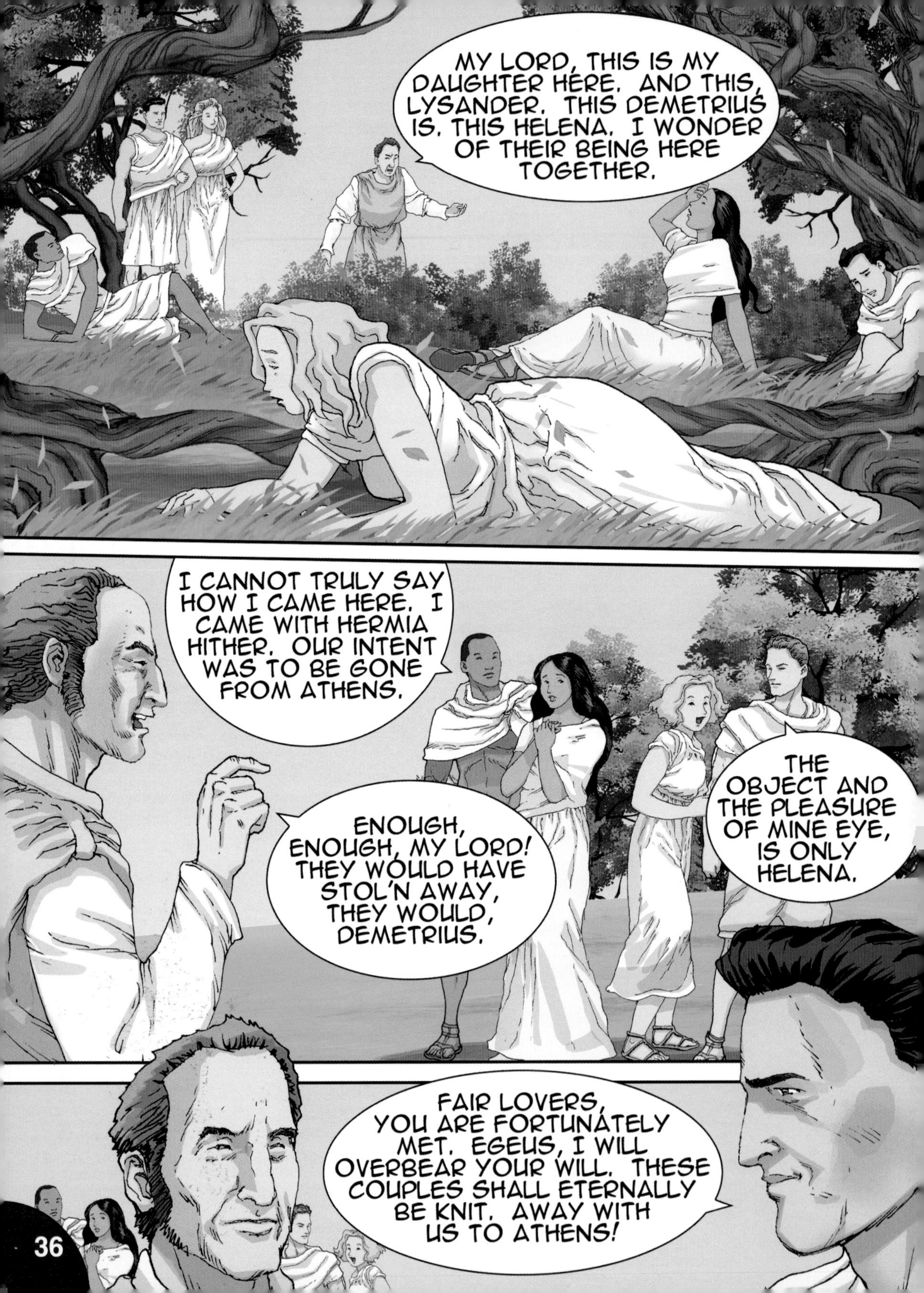
MY LORD, THIS IS MY DAUGHTER HERE. AND THIS, LYSANDER. THIS DEMETRIUS IS. THIS HELENA. I WONDER OF THEIR BEING HERE TOGETHER.
I CANNOT TRULY SAY HOW I CAME HERE. I CAME WITH HERMIA HITHER. OUR INTENT WAS TO BE GONE FROM ATHENS.
ENOUGH, ENOUGH, MY LORD! THEY WOULD HAVE STOL'N AWAY, THEY WOULD, DEMETRIUS.
THE OBJECT AND THE PLEASURE OF MINE EYE, IS ONLY HELENA.
FAIR LOVERS, YOU ARE FORTUNATELY MET. EGEUS, I WILL OVERBEAR YOUR WILL. THESE COUPLES SHALL ETERNALLY BE KNIT. AWAY WITH US TO ATHENS!

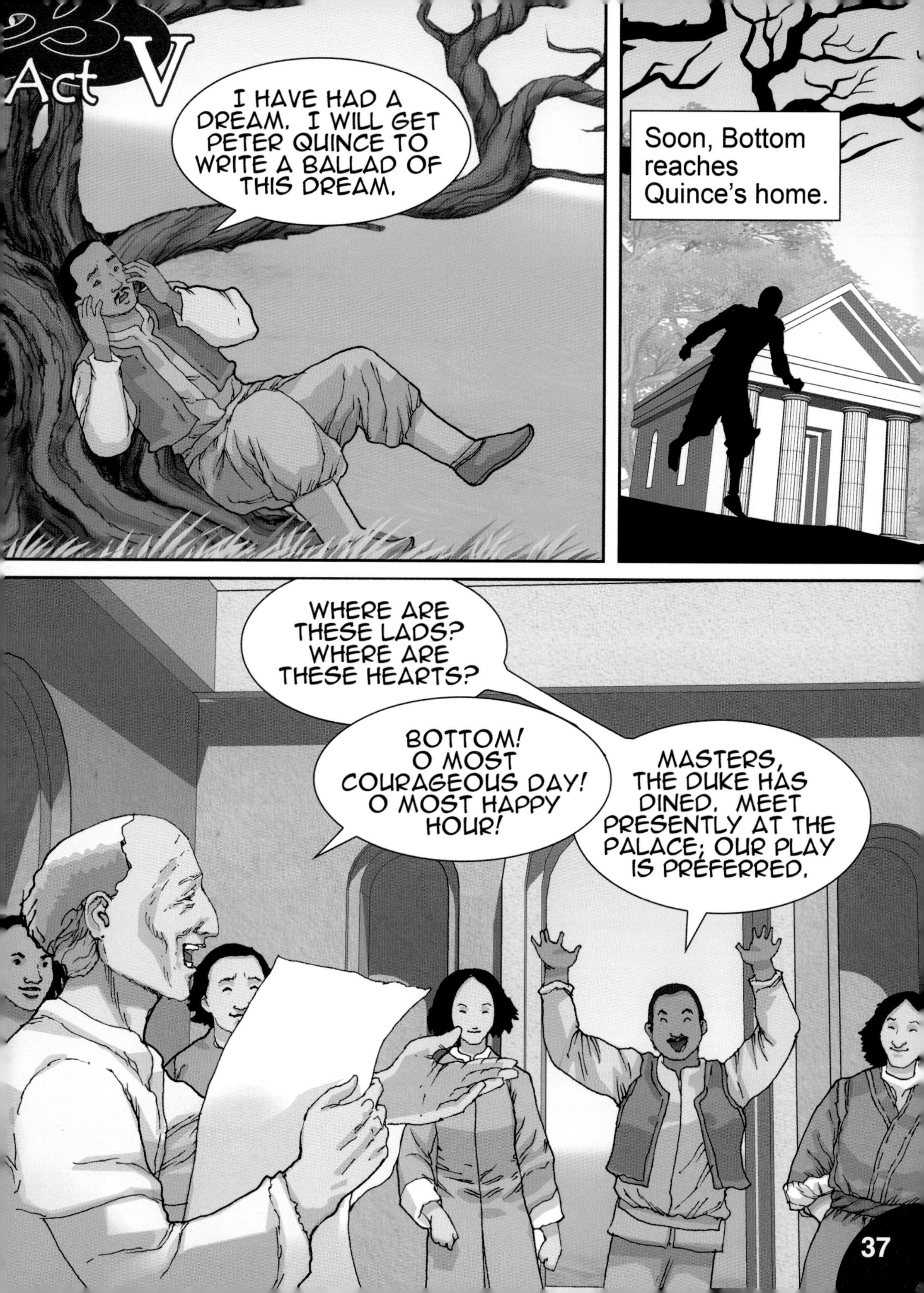
Act V
I HAVE HAD A DREAM. I WILL GET PETER QUINCE TO WRITE A BALLAD OF THIS DREAM.
Soon, Bottom reaches Quince's home.
WHERE ARE THESE LADS? WHERE ARE THESE HEARTS?
BOTTOM! O MOST COURAGEOUS DAY! O MOST HAPPY HOUR!
MASTERS, THE DUKE HAS DINED. MEET PRESENTLY AT THE PALACE; OUR PLAY IS PREFERRED.

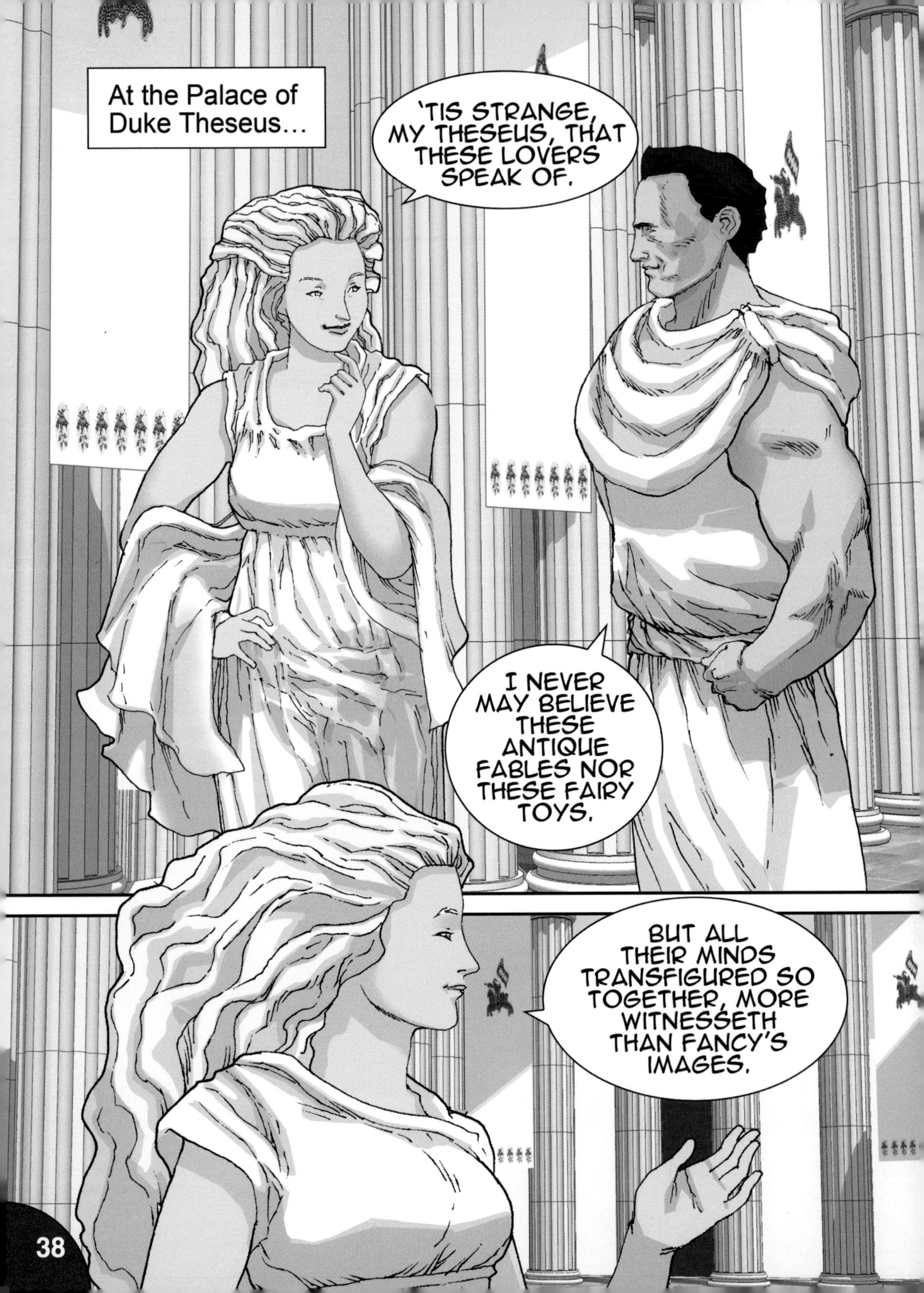

At the Palace of Duke Theseus...
'TIS STRANGE, MY THESEUS, THAT THESE LOVERS SPEAK OF.
I NEVER MAY BELIEVE THESE ANTIQUE FABLES NOR THESE FAIRY TOYS.
BUT ALL THEIR MINDS TRANSFIGURED SO TOGETHER, MORE WITNESSETH THAN FANCY'S IMAGES.

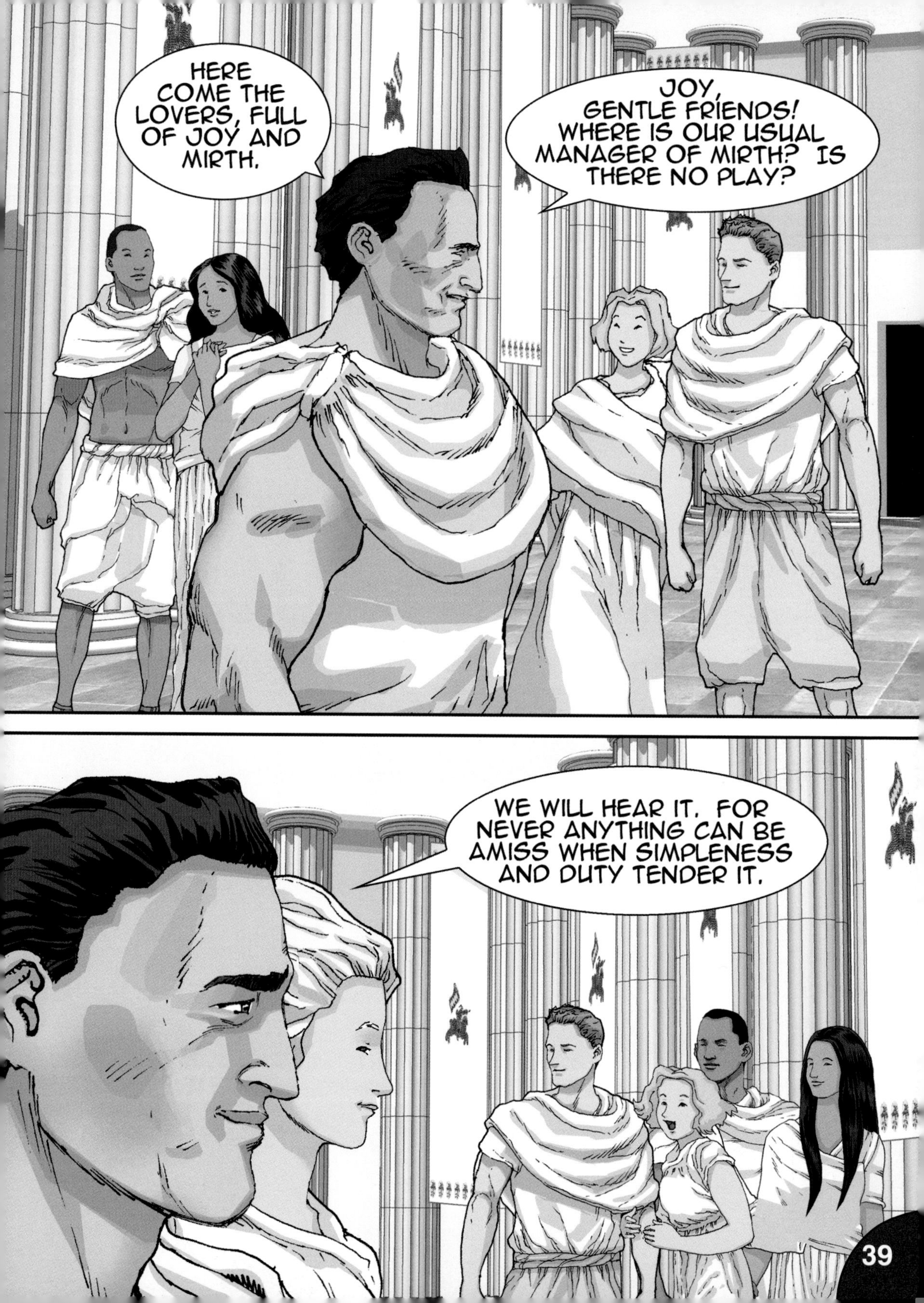
HERE COME THE LOVERS, FULL OF JOY AND MIRTH.
JOY, GENTLE FRIENDS! WHERE IS OUR USUAL MANAGER OF MIRTH? IS THERE NO PLAY?
WE WILL HEAR IT. FOR NEVER ANYTHING CAN BE AMISS WHEN SIMPLENESS AND DUTY TENDER IT.

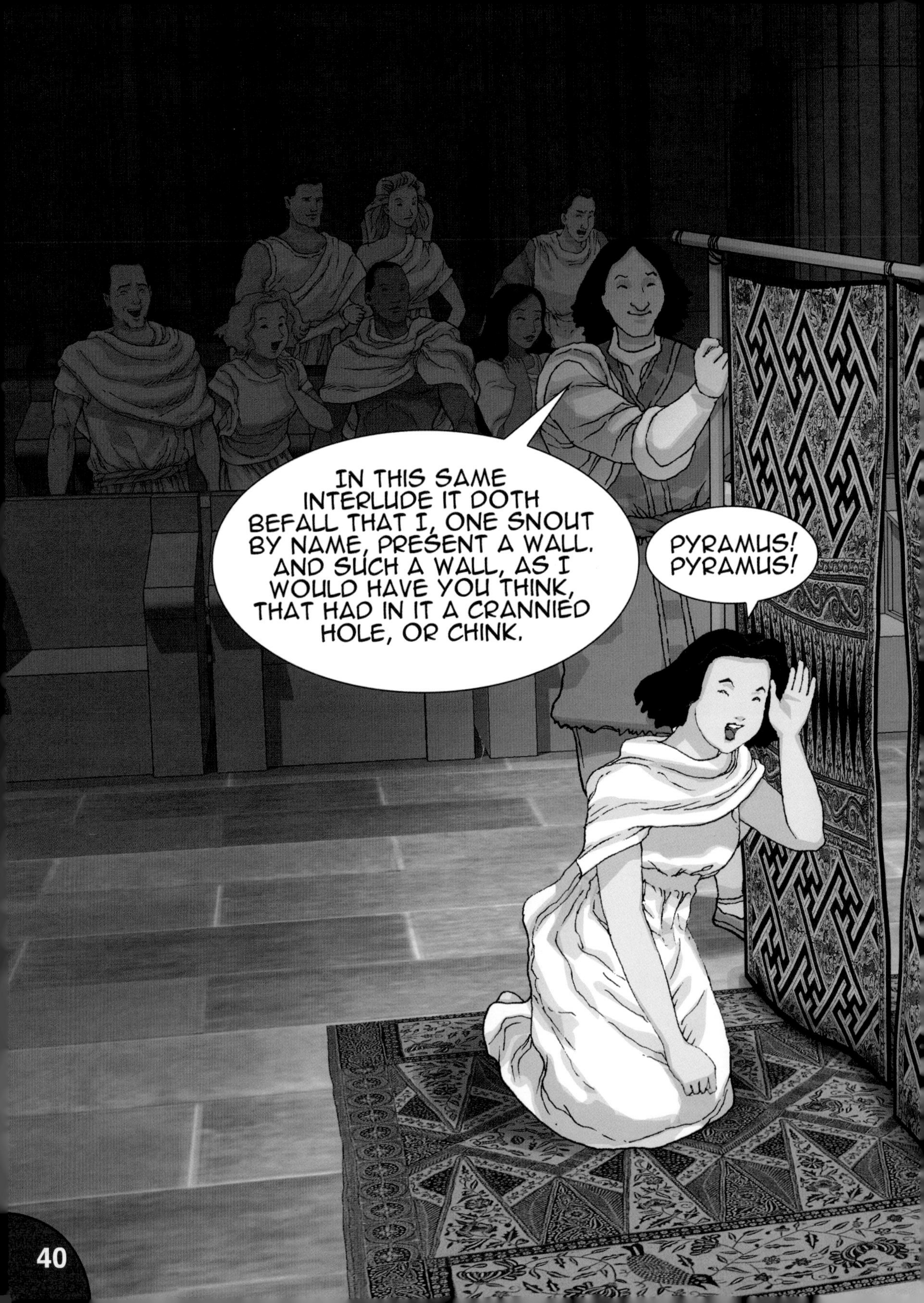
IN THIS SAME INTERLUDE IT DOTH BEFALL THAT I, ONE SNOUT BY NAME, PRESENT A WALL. AND SUCH A WALL, AS I WOULD HAVE YOU THINK, THAT HAD IN IT A CRANNIED HOLE, OR CHINK.
PYRAMUS! PYRAMUS!

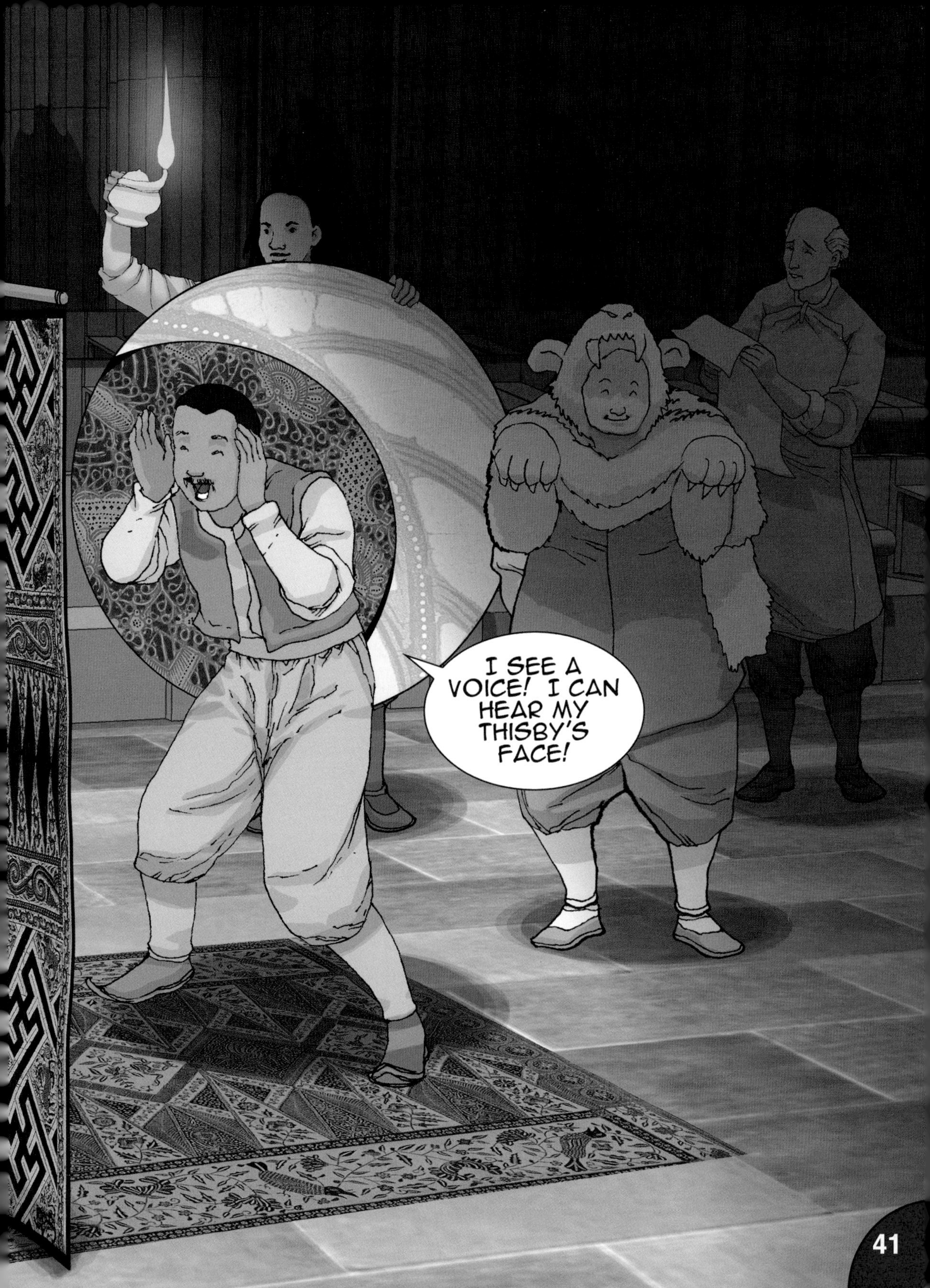
I SEE A VOICE! I CAN HEAR MY THISBY'S FACE!

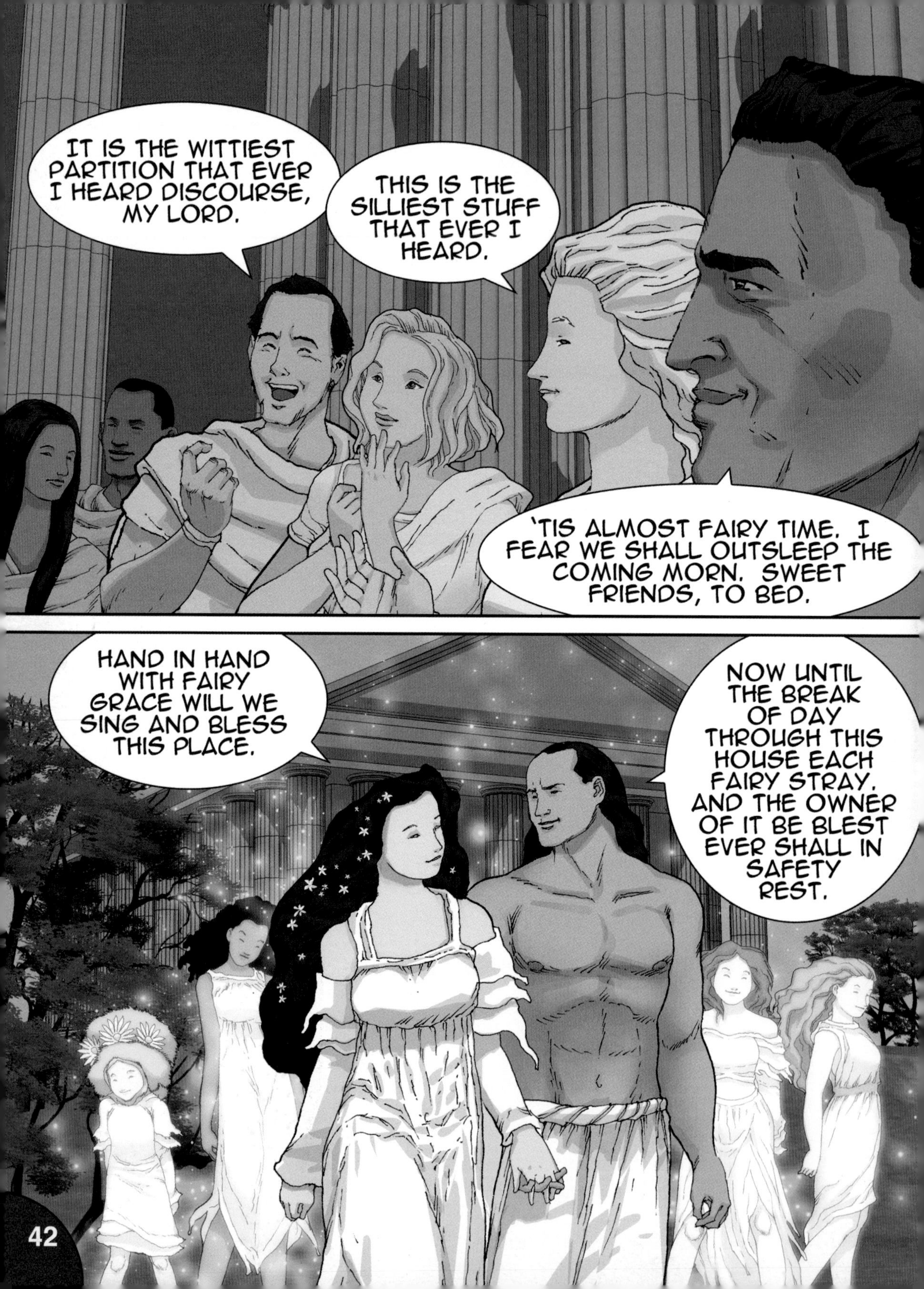
IT IS THE WITTIEST PARTITION THAT EVER I HEARD DISCOURSE, MY LORD.
THIS IS THE SILLIEST STUFF THAT EVER I HEARD.
'TIS ALMOST FAIRY TIME. I FEAR WE SHALL OUTSLEEP THE COMING MORN. SWEET FRIENDS, TO BED.
HAND IN HAND WITH FAIRY GRACE WILL WE SING AND BLESS THIS PLACE.
NOW UNTIL THE BREAK OF DAY THROUGH THIS HOUSE EACH FAIRY STRAY. AND THE OWNER OF IT BE BLEST EVER SHALL IN SAFETY REST.

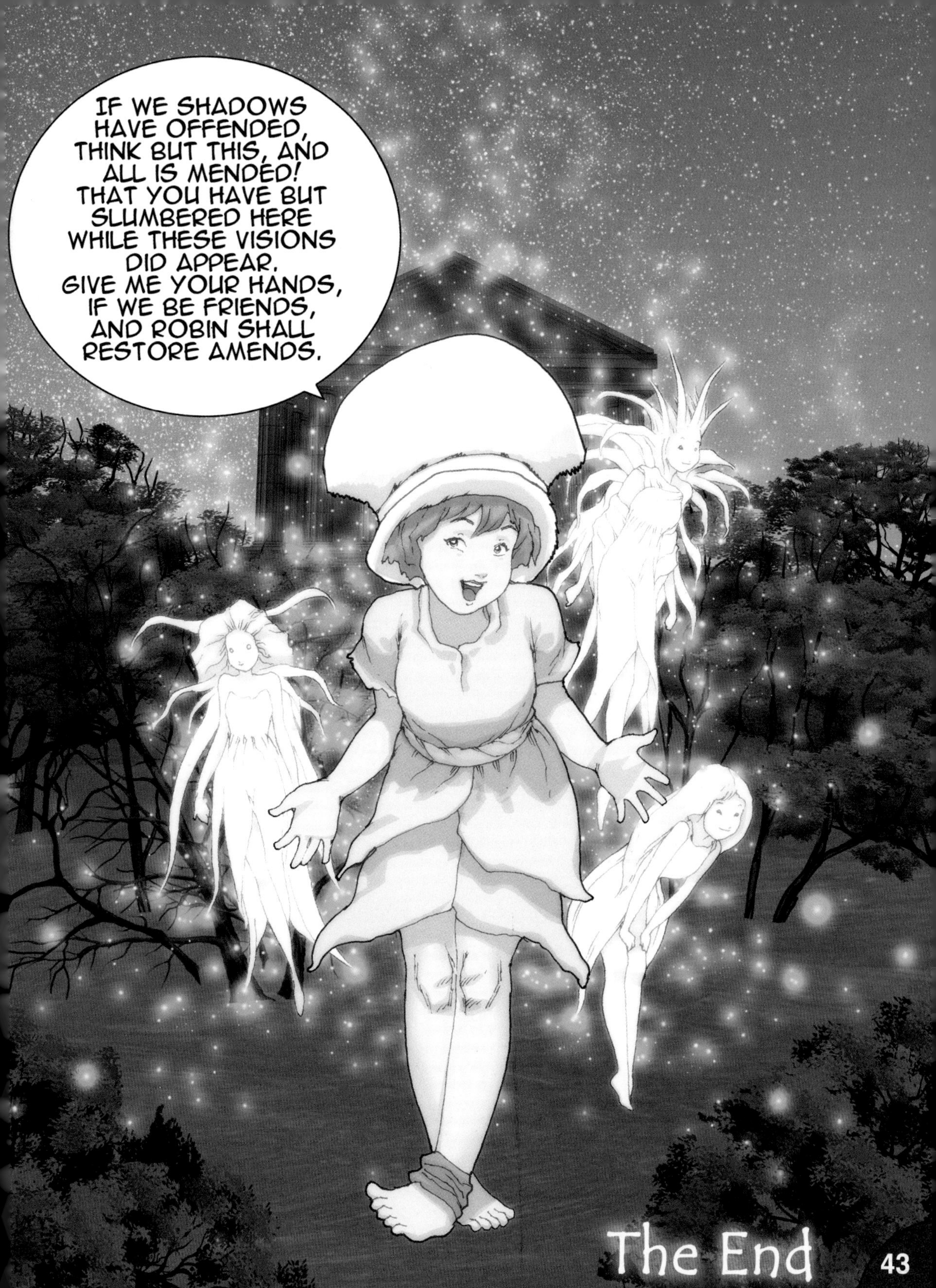
IF WE SHADOWS HAVE OFFENDED, THINK BUT THIS, AND ALL IS MENDED! THAT YOU HAVE BUT SLUMBERED HERE WHILE THESE VISIONS DID APPEAR. GIVE ME YOUR HANDS, IF WE BE FRIENDS, AND ROBIN SHALL RESTORE AMENDS.
The End

Behind A Midsummer Night's Dream

William Shakespeare wrote *A Midsummer Night's Dream* in 1595 or 1596. Shakespeare used multiple sources when writing the play. He drew on Greek mythology, English country fairy lore, and various texts.

A Midsummer Night's Dream is set in and around the city of Athens, Greece. The city lies in southeastern Greece, near the Aegean Sea. In the 400s BC, Athens was the world's most highly civilized city. Ancient Greeks built the city on and around a hill, which became known as the Acropolis. They constructed and decorated beautiful temples for gods and goddesses.

The play begins in Athens, where Theseus and Hippolyta prepare to be married. Meanwhile, a young couple, Hermia and Lysander, escape to the forest to avoid Hermia having to marry Demetrius. Demetrius and Helena enter the forest to find them.

In the forest, Oberon, king of the fairies, sends his servant, Puck, for a magic love potion. This potion will make Titania, queen of the fairies, fall in love with whatever person or creature she sees when she awakes.

Oberon also tells Puck to use the potion on Demetrius so that he will once again love Helena. By mistake, Puck uses the love potion on Lysander, who then falls in love with Helena. Now, both men are in love with Helena.

Meanwhile, a group of actors rehearse a play for Theseus's wedding. Puck gives Bottom, one of the actors, a donkey's head. Titania awakens and falls in love with Bottom. After much humorous confusion and misunderstanding, magic restores everyone to their normal states.

The play ends at the duke's wedding. The two couples are also married at the wedding. During the celebration, the actors perform their comical play.

The first performance of *A Midsummer Night's Dream* was most likely before 1598. The play was first published in 1600. It was again published in 1623 in the collected works of Shakespeare, called the *First Folio*. Today, the *First Folio* is the source for most of Shakespeare's plays. *A Midsummer Night's Dream* has been performed onstage throughout the world.

Famous Phrases

The course of true love never did run smooth.

I know a bank where the wild thyme blows,
Where oxlips and the nodding violet grows.

Lord, what fools these mortals be!

Love looks not with the eyes, but with the mind,
And therefore is winged Cupid painted blind.

Never did mockers waste more idle breath!

About the Author

William Shakespeare was baptized on April 26, 1564, in Stratford-upon-Avon, England. At the time, records were not kept of births, however, the churches did record baptisms, weddings, and deaths. So, we know approximately when he was born. Traditionally, his birth is celebrated on April 23.

William was the son of John Shakespeare, a tradesman, and Mary Arden. He most likely attended grammar school and learned to read, write, and speak Latin.

Shakespeare did not go on to the university. Instead, he married Anne Hathaway at age 18. They had three children, Susanna, Hamnet, and Judith. Not much is known about Shakespeare's life at this time. By 1592 he had moved to London, and his name began to appear in the literary world.

In 1594, Shakespeare became an important member of Lord Chamberlain's company of players. This group had the best actors and the best theater, the Globe. For the next 20 years, Shakespeare devoted himself to writing. He died on April 23, 1616, but his works have lived on.

Additional Works by Shakespeare

The Comedy of Errors (1589–94)
The Taming of the Shrew (1590–94)
Romeo and Juliet (1594–96)
A Midsummer Night's Dream (1595–96)
Much Ado About Nothing (1598–99)
As You Like It (1598–1600)
Hamlet (1599–1601)
Twelfth Night (1600–02)
Othello (1603–04)
King Lear (1605–06)
Macbeth (1606–07)
The Tempest (1611)

About the Adapters

Rod Espinosa has worked in advertising, software entertainment, and film. Today, he lives in San Antonio, Texas, and produces stunning graphic novels including *Dinowars, Neotopia, Metadocs, Battle Girls,* and many others. His graphic novel *Courageous Princess* was nominated for an Eisner Award and *Neotopia* was nominated for the Max und Moritz Award.

As a life long graphic novel and literature fan, Daniel Conner is thrilled to be a part of this graphic novel series. Other works of his, including musical endeavors, have appeared in various Graphic Novel anthologies, CDs, and Web sites. He is a high school teacher and small group leader at his church in San Antonio, TX, where he lives with his sensational wife, Hannah, and their cat.

dote - to show affection.

edict - an order or demand.

enamored - in love with.

eyne - a spelling of eyes that is used for rhyme.

girdle round about the earth - cover the earth searching.

glade - an open space surrounded by woods.

henchman - a page to a person of high rank.

hither - to this place.

knavery - being deceitful.

league - a measurement of distance.

love-in-idleness - the name for a pansy.

negligence - showing carelessness.

nuptial hour - time of our wedding.

weed - clothing

Web Sites

To learn more about William Shakespeare, visit ABDO Publishing Company on the World Wide Web at **www.abdopublishing.com**. Web sites about Shakespeare are featured on our Book Links page. These links are routinely monitored and updated to provide the most current information available.